Roadkill Café

Also written by C. L. Conolly

<u>Lone Titles</u>
Friendly Misfortunes
Killer Suburbia

<u>The Affair Series</u>
Forbidden Affair
Family Affair
Fundamental Affair
Fruitful Affair

<u>The Cult Series</u>
Disciples Doctrine
City of Disciples
Shunning of Disciples
Mutiny of Disciples
Disbanding of Disciples

Roadkill Café

C. L. Conolly

KILLER WORDS PUBLISHING
Cover art by C. L. Conolly

ROADKILL CAFÉ
ISBN - 978-1-963747-01-0

C. L. Conolly
www.clconolly.com
New Ulm, Texas

Printed in the United States of America

10 9 8 7 6 5 4 3 2 1

Never forbid your children from doing anything. Children want to be their own person. Forbidding them to do things, say things, or see people will only cause them to rebel and the results could be fatal.

One

There was a small town at the end of a road. It kept secrets…everyone's secrets, because it had secrets of its own. When Nicole met Armando she was trying to escape her toxic family. She was the oldest of eight children, so she was the throw away child.

Growing up, Nicole always wanted her parents to

divorce (or at least one of them to die), because she knew they were unhappy together. As she grew older, she figured they just enjoyed being miserable and that was why they stayed together. Nicole did everything to try and get noticed by her parents, but her father was an abusive drunk and her mother was a narcissist.

Nicole and Armando eloped in a courthouse wedding with only his family in attendance. She was nineteen, he was twenty six. He had been working since he was sixteen years old and had managed to save hundreds of thousands of dollars living with his parents.

Three months after they were married, they gathered his savings and moved to a small town named 'Friendly'. Due to the toxic home Nicole had grown up in, from the first time they had started dating, she had always told him she wanted to live around friendly people and as far away from her parents as possible. He was the one who found the town and it was the perfect place for them to live.

Friendly was quaint with a population of just under one thousand. Armando had found a rundown building across the road from a bustling motel that used to be the town restaurant. The original owner had died and Friendly was left without a local restaurant for five years. It wasn't a long drive to the nearest eatery, but it was inconvenient and most of the townsfolk would just cook at home.

The building was up for sale and even had a small single bedroom cabin behind it that was included in the sale price. Since Armando had never moved out of his parents home, he had saved up half a million dollars from the time he had his first job.

He had worked in fast food restaurants and retail. Beginning at the age of eighteen he had gone to work on an offshore oil rig. When he was twenty one, he chose to get a job working close to home in the refineries.

He had been making several thousands of dollars each week and since his work days were twelve to eighteen hours a day for three months straight, he didn't really have any time to go out and spend any of the money he made. Living with his parents through his twenties was only bearable in small increments, so he would only take seven days off between job assignments.

Since he had an abundant savings account, they were able to pay cash for the restaurant and moved into the cabin immediately. The restaurant required an extensive renovation process. They made sure to get to know all of the other local business owners and within six weeks, their business was ready to open.

Melanie was the owner of the motel directly across the street from the café. "Well, well, well. Nicole, y'all have done a great job getting this place back into working order. I can't wait to eat here. Are you going to invite your families to your grand opening?"

Nicole rolled her eyes. "I would rather stab myself in the eye with an extremely dull knife and wiggle it around."

Melanie giggled. "Wow. That was very graphic. Who's family is that aimed at?"

"Well," Nicole began, then let out a deep breath before she continued. "Armando's family doesn't own a reliable vehicle that could make the trip safely, so they wouldn't be able to make it. As for my family, my parents are manipulative, narcissistic and abusive - in all sense of the word. When I began dating Armando, he treated me the way I had always wished my parents would treat me; as if I was important in their lives."

"Damn. Are they really that bad?" Melanie wondered.

Nicole bit down on her bottom lip, then decided to tell her the story of her childhood. "The two people who should have been there to protect and love me unconditionally, treated me as though I was a burden from the age of two. The more children they had, the more I was shoved to the side. I was blamed for everything done in the house, even if I wasn't home at the time. My mother berated me and my father would throw me against the wall. By the time I was sixteen and could legally get a job, I was then treated as their personal ATM machine.

"At the end of my senior year in high school, I met Armando. We had only been together for three months when my parents decided having eight children living at home was too much and I was forced to move out as soon as possible. I still had eight weeks left before graduation and about fifteen weeks before I turned eighteen."

Melanie scoffed. "Why were they trying to shove you out of the house?"

Nicole rested her chin on her hand. "They wanted my room so the older of my four younger sisters could have her own room. I have four younger sisters and three little brothers who are the babies. The boys are triplets. I had my own room, the four other girls shared a room and the boys shared the largest room because they are my parents golden children.

"I found a place to move into and moved out of my parents house two months before my eighteenth birthday. It was a converted detached garage and the landlord was only charging me three hundred dollars a month for rent. Armando stayed over as much as he was able. If he wasn't working, he was at my place. My parents didn't like the fact that Armando and I were spending so much time together and I was no longer giving them money."

"They told you to leave. Why would they expect you to keep giving them money?" Melanie asked.

"My parents believe that their children are their property. Whatever I have, I have it because they allowed me to have it. I'm not stupid. I know better than that, so I immediately cut them off the second I left their house."

"Good. They sound like they don't deserve anything. Besides that, doesn't your dad have a job?"

"Sometimes he did and sometimes he didn't. My parents don't trust each other, so when my mother would accuse my dad of cheating, he would quit his job. He said it was so she could monitor his actions, but I knew it was because he believed she was also cheating."

"Why don't they just get a divorce?"

"Oh, absolutely not. My grandparents and my aunt have very happy marriages and my mother would never want to be the first one to get a divorce. She is too narcissistic to admit that she's the one ruining her marriage. My mother also can't stand the fact that she's miserable, but my aunt is following her dreams and has a wonderful life."

"Well, misery loves company. It sounds like she's more upset that no one else in the family is as miserable as she is, so she has to make everyone living in her home miserable," Melanie theorized. "So what made you decide to move out here?"

Nicole pursed her lips and curled the corners of her mouth up. "After I had been living on my own for six months, I was evicted. I didn't know why I was being evicted since I had always paid rent on time and all my bills were paid. When I was finally able to get ahold of the landlord to ask why, I was told that he had received a phone call that there was an unauthorized tenant living with me.

"I tried to explain that Armando wasn't living there, but the landlord didn't care and told me to go back to my parents' house. That was when I realized my mother was the one who called my landlord and she was the one who had got me evicted."

Melanie looked at Nicole with her mouth agape. "Damn. If she didn't want you in the house, why would she get you evicted?"

Nicole laid her arms down on the table in front of her and grabbed her elbows. "Because she doesn't like Armando."

"So what happened when you told your mom you

had been evicted?"

"Oh, when I informed my parents of the circumstances, I was told there wasn't any room for me at their house. My mother told me I could store my stuff at her house until I found a place to live, but other than that, I was no longer welcome to live with them."

"Where am I suppose to go?" Nicole asked her mother, as they moved her stuff back to her parents' house.

"Nicole, that is not my problem. You are eighteen. That means you are an adult. You need to figure this out on your own," her mother told her.

"I guess I will just move in with Armando then," Nicole said, as she headed out to her car.

"He is the reason you aren't allowed to live in my home anymore. If you move in with him, don't you dare ever come back. I will keep all your shit and you will have nothing!" Nicole's mother shouted at her, as she stood in the doorway.

"That's not fair. You can't just take my stuff because you don't like my boyfriend."

"Wanna bet? I know he is twenty five and you are only eighteen. I can call the cops and have him arrested."

"No you can't. Like you said, I'm an adult."

"I will lie and make sure he is arrested. He is trash and isn't good enough to be part of this family."

"Apparently, I'm not good enough to be part of this family either."

"Quit being a bitch, Nicole."

"You are a bitch, mother."

Melanie clapped her hands. "Hell yeah, girl! Good for you telling her off."

Nicole shrugged. "It gets worse. I drove away from her house and called Armando as I tried to find out where I would stay. Unfortunately, he was at work, so he didn't answer the phone. That day, I ended up driving around for a couple of hours before going back to my parents' house."

"Why would you go back?"

"When I had arrived back to my parents' house, no one was home and the door was locked. I knew no one would be there because my mother had to pick up my siblings from school. She didn't allow them to ride the bus. She had taken the house key away from me when I moved out, but I knew which window didn't lock and I made my way around to the side of the house.

"I climbed into the window and sat down on the sofa in the living room, waiting for my mother to return from picking up my siblings from school. After forty five minutes, I heard the children yelling from outside on the driveway. I didn't get up, or move from the spot on the sofa.

"My mother never let us kids play outside, so when no one had come into the house after twenty minutes, I got up and opened the front door. I had left my car parked in the driveway, so she knew I was there. She had called the cops and I saw four officers speaking with her when I opened the door."

"Your mother sounds like a raging bitch. What did the police do?"

"Put your hands up and slowly walk toward me," an officer ordered Nicole, aiming his weapon at her.

"What the hell is going on?" Nicole asked, raising her hands over her head and walking toward him.

"Ma'am, you are under arrest for breaking and entering," the officer told her, putting his gun away and hooking his handcuffs on her wrists behind her back.

"This is my parents' house."

"And when you made entrance into the home, your parents were not here. Your mother informed us that you no longer live here and were not welcome here."

"Are you fucking kidding me? Mom, this is a shitty thing to do to your oldest child. Just because you don't like my boyfriend, you are literally going to have me arrested for being at your house?"

Nicole's mother wouldn't even look at her, nor speak to her. She just stood over by her vehicle and talked to the other officers.

"She isn't suppose to be here, because her boyfriend threatened to kill us. We would like for her to distance herself from this man. When she decides that she would like to be part of this family again, without that horrible man, then she will be welcome in the home. I have seven other children to protect," Nicole's mother lied to

the police.

"Armando has NEVER threatened you in any way! Stop trying to manipulate this situation and justify your actions. You are a shitty mother and no matter what you try to pretend to be won't change that," Nicole yelled at her.

Melanie leaned back and rubbed her hands on her thighs. "Holy Shit! Your mother had you arrested and lied about Armando?"

Nicole half shrugged. "My mother has this stupid thing she does when she is trying to manipulate people into feeling bad for her. She presses the tips of her thumb and forefinger to the tip of her nose, closes her eyes and focuses real hard to force herself to cry. Sometimes she pinches the bridge of her nose right between her eyes, or puts four fingers against her mouth. It's what she always does in order to gain sympathy from others who don't know her personally. Those of us who know her, know that she's faking and don't give a shit. I don't even think she has any real feelings other than anger and hate."

Melanie groaned. "Ewww. I don't even know her and I already hate her. So what happened with the cops?"

"They asked her if she wanted to press charges against me for breaking into her home. She sniffed to go with the façade of her fake crying and in a low sullen tone, while patting the sides of her eyes with her finger tips she told them to let me go. She said she just wanted me off her property. The cop took the handcuffs off and I asked if I could speak with my sisters Monica and Erin. Monica is seventeen and next in line to get a job and start giving my mother money and Erin is fifteen. Erin is opinionated, which is awesome because she will mouth off to my parents. I was closer to them due to shared parental trauma. Monica has been having trouble keeping up with funding my mother's spending habits. Every time she tries to save a little money, so she can move out when she graduates, but my mother forces her to hand it over. As for Erin, she has always basically been ignored by my parents.

"When my mother found out she was having a third girl, she debated with the idea of an abortion. My parents wanted a boy so desperately, they continued having children until they finally had one. Of course they ended up with an identical set of triplets for their boy. Unfortunately, it wasn't until babies number six, seven and eight that they were able to have their son and by then, the damage to their girls had already been done. Monica and Erin were the only two sisters I feel like I have actually grown up with because after Erin, my parents waited eight years before having any more kids."

Melanie sighed and shook her head. "I felt bad for you in the beginning, but you were able to get away from that bitch. Now I feel bad for your siblings. Especially Erin. She seems like a sweet kid that has to defend herself everyday. So did your mom let you talk to them?"

Nicole nodded. "My mother nodded her head without saying a word and Monica and Erin slowly walked toward me. Before she went into the house, my mother thanked the police officers for their assistance, still pretending to cry, then she took my five youngest siblings, Tiffany seven, Brittney five and Johnny, Jimmy and Joe the three year old triplets, into the house. I waited until the front door had closed behind my mother before I said anything to my sisters.

"I don't know what is going to happen, but I promise I will come back for y'all."

"Please don't leave us here. I don't know how you were able to go to school and work two jobs. Mom says I will have to get a second job because dad wants a new truck," Monica told her.

"That is not your responsibility. Stop paying their bills," Nicole assured her.

"What would they have done if you did that?" Monica asked.

"Dad would have held me against the wall by my throat and mom would have told me it was my fault he treated me that way. Okay, your right. Just don't get a second job," Nicole said.

"Take me with you," Erin begged.

"If I could, I would. If mom would call the cops on me for just going inside the house when she's not home, I would definitely go to jail for kidnapping if I took you with me," Nicole told Erin, cupping her face in her

hands.

"How do we get out of here. I don't think I can wait another eleven months," Monica said.

"My mother opened the front door and stood in the doorway. The officer who had cuffed me stayed behind to watch me. As my mother leaned against the doorframe with her arms crossed under her boobs, the cop finally told me I needed to leave and my sisters had to go inside."

Melanie rolled her eyes and scoffed. "I know that stance. It's the bitch stance. Those women who push their arms up under their tits because they think it makes them seem more authoritative. So what happened?"

"I hugged my two sisters and cried. I needed a plan to get them away from the abusive home they lived in and do what I could to show them how important they really are. Erin was the one I was mostly worried about. She had told me when she was ten that she thought about killing herself because our parents didn't want her anyway. I always told her I loved her and that I needed her.

"Monica and Erin slowly walked up to the front door and disappeared inside the house. I made my way to my car and started it up. The police drove off and I backed out of the driveway. As I drove down the street, still not knowing where I was going to go, my phone rang. It was Armando.

"Babe, what am I going to do?" Nicole cried, into the phone.

"What happened?" Armando asked.

Nicole told him about the entire exchange with her mother, tears streaming down her face. By the time she had finished, she was crying so hard, she had to pull over.

"That fucking bitch! Don't worry babe, we will fig-ure something out. I will take care of those two ass-holes," Armando told her.

"I don't have anywhere to live."

"Yes you do. You can live at my house."

"You still live with your parents. Would they be okay if I moved in with you?"

"They won't notice and I will find us somewhere to live, just the two of us."

"Can it be far away from my parents?"

"We will go where ever you want to go."

"I love you, babe."

"Love you too, babe."

"That was it. Armando and I have been together ever since and all we have thought about was how we would be able to get at least Monica and Erin away from my parents. I don't really know Tiffany, Brittney, Joe, Jimmy or Johnny, but I know my brothers are being raised as spoiled brats." Nicole looked down at her lap and held back tears. "I never told anyone else that story except Armando. It's hard reliving the shit I went through growing up and the fact that my sisters are still there."

Bernard spoke from the doorway of the café. "Don't worry, Nicole. We can come up with something to eliminate your parents and save your siblings. Marvin and I were working with the last owner of this place. Get Armando. I think we should talk."

Two

Bernard followed Nicole out the back door to the cabin. Armando chose to renovate the café first, so they could begin making money before he started on the cabin. Since the café was two weeks away from the grand opening, he had decided to work on the cabin during the times that all they were waiting for was a delivery for the grand opening.

Nicole peeked in the open front door. Armando was sanding the floors before he rolled on the sealant, so she had to yell over the sound of the power sander. "Hey, babe."

Armando's head snapped in her direction. His eyes were wide open with surprise. He let out a deep breath, as he switched off the floor sander. "Babe! You spooked me. What's up?"

Nicole hitched her thumb over her shoulder. "Bernard says he wants to help with my siblings and he wants us to meet up with Marvin as well."

Her husband shrugged, unplugged the power sander and walked out the front door of the cabin to join them at the picnic area between the two buildings. Bernard and Melanie were already sitting at the table. Armando brushed the sawdust off his clothing before he sat down next to his wife.

Bernard patted his hand on the table in front of Nicole. "When was the last time you spoke to your sisters?"

She shrugged, genuinely not being able to remember. "My mother blocked me from being able to contact Monica and Erin. She told me that I was corrupting my siblings with my lies about my parents. I don't have to lie to my siblings about my parents. My sisters know how shitty they are first hand. The worst part is that my mother won't admit that she is doing anything wrong. She knows exactly what she is doing. The house motto is, 'What happens at home, stays at home'. That's because she doesn't want any of the kids asking for help."

"You should invite your family to your grand opening," Bernard suggested.

"Why the fuck would I do that?" Nicole asked, curling her upper lip.

Bernard raised his eyebrows. "You could potentially incorporate them into the restaurant."

Nicole looked at him confused. "What are you talking about? My parents are too lazy to work. They would rather have their children work for them."

Marvin walked up from around the side of the café. "Not for them to work, but they could feed several people each."

Nicole turned around to face the owner of the

town's only gas station and mechanic shop. "They literally won't even serve food to their own children. I know for a fact they won't serve food to strangers."

Marvin tilted his head down, raised his eyebrows and flashed her a sly smile. "Oh, I'm not talking about them physically serving food. If you grind them up, I bet your dad could feed a couple hundred and your mom could feed a little over a hundred. Do you remember the first time we met and I asked you about your family? You were vague about your childhood and who your parents were as people, but you had no problem telling me about their physical appearances."

Nicole shrugged. "Both my mother and father are well overweight, whereas all of the kids living in the house are basically malnourished. Erin is the one I'm mainly concerned about because she is extremely boney. Breakfast is nonexistent for the kids, except my brothers get candy if they tell my mother they're hungry. The kids only get lunch on the days they go to school because they get free lunch. At home, my mother will put butter on a piece of bread and the kids get butter bread and water for lunch. Six nights a week, dinner is whatever the kids can make for themselves. Most of the time it's just a bowl of cereal, as long as it's not the cereal my parents bought specifically for themselves. If we ate their cereal, we were beat with the metal end of the belt that hangs in the living room."

Bernard reached across the table and touched Nicole's hand. "You know how we had the conversation about mixing wildlife meat with the beef delivery as filler in order to stretch out the order? People are meat. We could mix them in with the beef as well."

Nicole pulled her hands off the table and placed them in her lap. "Is that even legal? Or ethical? What would the residents say if they knew they were eating human meat?"

Marvin stepped up behind Nicole and placed one hand on her shoulder. "I know Bernard probably told you that we used to work with the last owner of the café. Melanie was the first step in that partnership. As a matter of fact, sometimes Betty from the boutique would let Mel know there was a potential meat sack heading her way to stay in the motel."

Armando shifted in his seat to turn and face Marvin.

"What do you mean by meat sack?"

Melanie bounced in her seat and smiled. "When a rude bitch comes through our town, they never leave. If they come into contact with Betty at the boutique and are rude to her, she asks them if they are staying in town. If they are staying at my motel, there is a special room I put them in. Marvin and Bernard then come in, take the fresh meat and they are brought over to the café to be cut up and ground into hamburger meat to be mixed in with the beef. I'd get rid of any vehicle left in my parking lot. By the time the previous owner of the café Gary died, I think the meat was less cow and more filler."

Bernard nodded. "Absolutely. If you were serving straight beef, the locals would be disappointed with the taste. As a matter of fact, they are the best to bring you fresh roadkill and would be happy to help if you ask."

Nicole looked over and made eye contact with Armando. "What do you think about this plan?"

Armando smiled and half shrugged. "It could be perfect. They would disappear and no one would know, except the two of us. We won't even tell your siblings."

"They would know that something is wrong. The control my mother craves over 'HER' family means she won't even let them out of her sight," Nicole said.

"I can set aside two motel rooms for them. One for just your parents and one for the kids," Melanie mentioned.

"HA!" Nicole began. "I don't think my mother likes my father that much to want to be alone with him. She prefers to have my three year old brothers in the bed with her."

Melanie opened her eyes wide and curled her upper lip. "Gross. Just ask and see if you can get them here. After that, we will figure it out."

Armando grabbed Nicole's hand. "We have that huge freezer where we can store them. As a matter of fact, if they come and actually stay the night, after your siblings go to bed, we can lock them in the freezer and leave them there until we are sure they are ready for processing."

Nicole looked around at everyone who were all smiling at her. Melanie was grinning from ear to ear, way too excited about the possibility of murdering

Nicole's parents. Bernard had a hopeful smile and his head tilted to the side, whereas Marvin's grin was a little more sly with his eyes wide. She took a deep breath, before she nodded, then pulled out her cell phone and texted her mother. '*Hey mom, Armando and I are opening a restaurant and we would like to invite all of you to come to the grand opening. We moved to a small town named Friendly.*'

It didn't take long before she responded. '*That's a far drive. I don't know if we can make it. The kids have school.*'

Nicole tried to call her, but she didn't answer the phone. She knew that meant that her mother was still mad at her and didn't want to hear her voice, so she just texted her again, since she was responding to that. '*It's on Saturday. The kids don't have school on the weekend.*'

The three dots popped up, indicating that she was typing a response. Nicole watched as the dots danced on the screen before disappearing. The thought went through her mind that her mother was probably telling her dad and complaining about having to drive so far.

Eventually, her response was received. *That's a six hour round trip drive. We would waste an entire day.'*

Nicole fought the urge to throw her phone and responded. *'There is a motel right across the street that y'all could stay in. It could be like a mini vacation. I haven't seen y'all for months and I miss my family.'*

Going back and forth over text message with her mother making excuses was making her so angry. Armando was being too nice by locking them into the freezer until they died. Nicole wanted to plunge a knife into her mother's neck. She couldn't stab her in the heart because her mother didn't have one and she knew there was a major artery in her neck that would kill her quickly.

'We don't have any money to pay to stay in a motel and we can't afford to pay for meals for everyone.' She continued with her excuses.

'Armando and I will make sure y'all are fed and we will pay for the motel. As a matter of fact, we will pay for 2 separate rooms, so you and dad can have your own room.' Nicole texted her.

'Fine' was the last thing she texted.

"Fucking bitch!" Nicole yelled, slamming her hand down on the table.

"What did she say?" Armando asked.

"They are coming, maybe. She said 'fine', so I guess that means they are coming," she told him, shrugging.

Marvin patted her shoulder. "We will take care of this, I promise."

Nicole rubbed her face with her hands. "I want to stab the bitch."

Armando grabbed his wife's hand again and gazed into her eyes. "The only reason I said to freeze them to death, is because it's the least messy way. If you stab them, there is blood to clean up. At least with my idea there isn't a messy clean up."

Melanie wiggled in her seat. "How long do you think it would take for them to freeze to death?"

Armando shrugged his shoulders. "I don't know, but I think if we turn it to as cold as it will go, it shouldn't take too long. We will just leave them in there overnight and check in the morning."

Nicole looked over at her husband. "What if they

are still alive in the morning?"

Bernard tapped the table with his middle finger as he spoke. "Putting them in the freezer overnight would slow them down if you have to stab them in the morning."

Armando wrapped his arms around his wife's shoulders and pulled her into him. "If they are still alive in the morning, you can stab the bitch in the neck and I will slit your dad's throat."

"Wouldn't it just be easier to kill them and clean up before my siblings wake up, just so we know they are dead?" Nicole asked, not wanting to wait and see if the cold kills them.

"If it makes you feel better, how about we just lock them in there for a couple of hours just to slow them down, then we can slit their throats. That way we can clean it up before your siblings get up in the morning and you won't have to wonder if they are dead, or just pissed off and cold," Armando reassured her.

"Thanks, babe," Nicole said, giving him a kiss. "One thing we are going to have to figure out is what we are going to do with all those kids once my parents are gone."

Armando rubbed his scruffy chin. "We can take in the two older ones, but the five younger ones, they may need to go with your grandmother or foster care. There is no way in hell I want to take care of the spawn of satan."

Three

When the day came for their grand opening, the whole town came in support of the new restaurant owners. Armando and Nicole had decided to name their eatery 'The Roadkill Café' due to the random raccoons and opossums found wandering around the property. Of course, they didn't inform their patrons as to whether or not those critters were mixed into the ground beef, or another type of critter was being used as filler meat.

"Nicole, this place looks great," Melanie, told her, as she walked into the café.

Nicole knew her mother, Jessica, would complain about how disgustingly dirty the restaurant was, so she was ferociously cleaning. "Thank you, Mel. Has my family checked in at the motel yet?"

Melanie shrugged. "As a matter of fact, Fran was checking in a couple with seven children when I was heading over here, so maybe."

"Nice to know they would rather check to see if I actually reserved them the two rooms, before coming over to see me," Nicole said, rolling her eyes.

"They could just want to put their bags in the rooms first."

"Keep that positive mindset when you actually meet my parents. They are so toxic."

"Well, did you need any help setting up before the crowd shows up?"

"Armando is prepping the meat for burgers, but what do you think if we were to set up a cold bar in order for our customers to build their own burgers?"

"I think that would be awesome! Do you have a cold bar?"

"We do. It's stored in the shed out back. Armando figured we could get the burgers out faster if the customers put their extras on themselves, but I wasn't really a fan, so I stored it out back."

"Does it work?" Melanie asked.

Nicole led her out to the back shed. "Oh yeah, it works. As a matter of fact, it's brand new. I just thought full service was better than self serve."

Melanie skipped in circles around Nicole. "Quick food and being able to fix it up how they want, is better than having complaints because there are so many customized orders for Armando to fill and it's taking too long. I know you have been advertising on social media and both Fran and I have been advertising for y'all both on social media as well as telling everyone who has checked into the motel. I know that a lot of the locals have been telling their tourists who have come into their shops."

Nicole clapped her fingers together. "It would be

awesome if we sold out today. We do have a beef order set to be delivered in the morning, but if we ran out of what we have for today, I think I might cry."

Melanie assisted Nicole with the cold bar, situating it in the perfect place, up near the area where the food pick-up was located. Armando and Nicole wanted to be able to run the restaurant theirselves at first, without having to hire too many employees. They felt as though, in the beginning, they wanted to be able to build rapport with the town and any visitors that came their way, before adding extras.

As Melanie and Nicole were filling the cold bar with ice, Jessica's irritated tone of voice bellowed from the front door. "Okay Nicole, we're here. Was there supposed to be some sort of party you were planning on throwing for us to drive all the way out here?"

Jessica walked over to a table followed by her father, Jerry, then her seven siblings behind them. Nicole rolled her eyes at Melanie, as the two of them were filling burger toppers and condiments, before she faked a smile a turned toward her family.

"Hello, mother. So glad y'all were able to make it,"

Nicole replied.

"Well, it looks like your business is already a failure. There isn't anyone here except you and your employee. Where is Armon?" Jessica said.

"First, this is Melanie. She is not my employee, she is the manager of the motel across the street. Second..." she began, before Jessica cut her off.

"Oh, so you actually belong across the street. Maybe you should go do your job at your own business, rather than doing Nicole's job at her business. She's an adult and needs to learn to work for her money," Jessica told Melanie.

Melanie started going off on Jessica. "Excuse me? Who the hell do you think you are?"

Nicole grabbed Melanie's arm and just shook her head. She knew that no matter what Melanie said, Jessica was going to pop off and say some stupid shit.

"You are disrespectful. Didn't your mother raise you to be respectful to your elders?" Jessica spat, stepping toward Melanie as if she was going to fight her.

"Hey Mel, can you go grab some tomatoes from the back? I believe Armando has already sliced them and packed them into containers that will fit directly into the cold bar," Nicole asked her, before the situation escalated any further.

"Sure I will. I wouldn't want to have to fight an elderly woman," Melanie said, as she walked toward the back, making eye contact with Jessica the whole way, squinting with rage.

"I don't think we will be staying long. I don't want to stay at a motel with someone like that running it," Jessica said, crossing her arms under her breasts.

"I thought you were here to support me, your daughter, not to make friends. Also, you know that Armando hates it when you call him Armon. Sometimes I feel like you do that on purpose, knowing that he hates it," Nicole scolded her.

Jerry and all seven of Nicole's siblings stood next to the table where Jessica was sitting. They were having to wait for Jessica to give them the okay to sit, so they wouldn't get yelled at for just existing.

"His full name is so long. It's just easier to shorten it," Jessica said, rolling her eyes.

"Look, I don't want to argue with you. I invited all

of you here to support my business. So, if you just want to complain, then go home. I know that the kids probably haven't had a good meal in a while and I also have offered to give y'all free food. If you want to leave and spend money at a fast food restaurant to stuff your face while the kids sit in the back of the vehicle smelling the food, just so they can have buttered bread when they get home, fine," Nicole told her mother, condescendingly.

"I don't know why you are saying those things to me, Nicole. I have done everything for you kids. I am always there anytime one of you needs me." She began her fake cry. "You have always been so ungrateful for everything your father and I have done for you."

Nicole rolled her eyes as Jessica lowered her head and pinched the bridge of her nose, taking a deep breath as she continued her crying façade. Jerry walked around the table to embrace Jessica, wrapping his arms around her shoulders.

Nicole turned toward her seven siblings, who were standing next to the table with their hands down by their sides and their heads down. "We technically don't open for another half an hour, but if y'all are hungry, I'm sure Armando wouldn't mind making a few burgers early."

"Sit!" Jessica ordered them, with a tone still indicative that she was attempting to cry. "Only three, they can share."

"Why can't they have their own burgers? That seems unfair," Nicole said, turning back toward Jessica.

Jerry rubbed one hand up and down Jessica's back and pointed a finger at his eldest daughter. "Could you please stop arguing with your mother and for once in your life, do what you're told."

Nicole threw her hands up in the air in defeat and headed to the back. Melanie hadn't come back out and Nicole knew it was because she didn't want to be around Jessica. At that point, *Nicole* didn't want to be around Jessica.

Armando and Melanie were in the back, prepping for the opening and talking about Nicole's mother. She knew Jessica was hard to deal with, but she always seemed to be nicer to people who weren't related to her. Jessica wanted to give off the illusion in order to make everyone believe she was a good person, even though she would talk shit about everyone behind their backs.

"Melanie tells me that your mother has already started with the rude comments," Armando said, when he saw Nicole appear from around the corner.

"Her narcissistic personality is really making an appearance today," his wife began, taking a deep breath in order to calm down before continuing. "Are you able to make three burgers, two split for two and one cut in thirds?"

"Jessica doesn't want to feed her children full meals I see. I will cut two burgers in half and one burger in thirds, placing each burger in their own basket, then fill the rest of the basket with fries, just for the kids to enjoy," Armando told Nicole, winking.

"Thanks, babe. I know the kids would enjoy that," she said, stepping up on her tip toes in order to kiss him on his cheek.

Nicole grabbed a container of tomatoes, a container of onions and a container of lettuce before heading back out to the front. As she stepped out into the seating area, it was empty. Jessica, Jerry and the kids were gone. Nicole walked over to the cold bar and placed the containers down into a few empty spaces.

Knowing that Jessica had walked away wanting Nicole to go find her so she could apologize to her, the eldest daughter took a deep breath, sucked it up and headed out of the café to find them. The second she stepped out onto the front patio, she could hear the shrill tone in Jessica's voice as she was arguing with Jerry.

"I DIDN'T WANT TO COME HERE ANYWAY! SHE HAS ALWAYS BEEN SO DISRESPECTFUL!" Jessica's voice echoed, from around the side of the building where the patio seating was located.

"Jessica, don't you want to be the bigger person and be here to support your daughter?" Jerry's voice was calm and he was trying to reason with his wife.

"NO, JERRY! SHE NEEDS TO APOLOGIZE IF SHE WANTS ME TO STAY!" Jessica continued to argue.

Nicole rubbed her forehead before stepping around the corner. Her siblings were sitting at one of the tables in the same position they had been sitting inside. Both of her parents turned towards her. Jessica's face was bright red and if it was possible, she would have had smoke billowing from her ears.

"Look, I just want to apologize for my attitude. I'm sorry, mom. Will y'all please come back inside? Armando is making food for the kids and I really want y'all to be here," Nicole told her, in her most sincere tone.

"There, was that so hard?" Jessica said, as she walked past her eldest daughter pursing her lips and holding her head with her nose pointed up.

Nicole balled her hands into fists and slammed both hands against her forehead. Jessica went inside and Jerry followed in behind her like the dog he was. Her siblings hadn't moved from their position at the table. If Nicole hadn't seen them walk into the restaurant initially, she would have assumed her parents were carrying around their dead bodies in order to keep up appearances.

"Hey guys. What the hell is going on?" Nicole asked, as she joined her siblings at the table.

"We were told not to talk to you," Erin told Nicole without moving.

"Why were you told not to talk to me?" Nicole

wanted to know.

"Because, Nicole. You left the house and mom no longer wants you to know any of the shitty things that happen at home. You just left us there to endure their abuse. I'm being forced to get two jobs, so I can pay their bills, just like you did. It's not fair and you don't exactly come by on a regular basis to visit. You moved further away and opened your own business just so you could have an excuse not to come by the house," Monica told her.

Nicole was glad that Monica at least looked up at her. She also slammed her hand down on the table. Monica and Erin knew how to make their older sister feel bad about leaving them behind, because she was the closest to those two. Tiffany and Brittney were toddlers when Nicole started working and she hadn't spent a lot of time with the triplets after they were born. For most of their short lives she was either at school, or at work, so she never really got to know them.

"I have a plan to help y'all out. Do you trust me?" Nicole asked, touching Monica's hand.

"Whatever. I'll believe it, when I see it," Monica

said, pulling her hand away from her sister, standing and walking toward the doors of the restaurant.

Nicole took a deep breath, stood, left the others sitting at the table and followed her sister around the corner. Monica opened the door and lowered her head, before asking Jessica if her and the others could come inside. She nodded, without looking up and headed back over to where the other children were still sitting.

Monica stood where they could see her and she snapped her fingers to get their attention. "Come on, we can go inside, but we aren't allowed to talk to, nor look at anyone."

Nicole followed them inside, as they returned to the same table and sat in the same position. Walking past her family, she stepped up to the food window just as Armando placed the burger baskets up for pick up. She picked up one in her right hand, balanced another on her forearm, then grabbed the third with her left hand.

"Here y'all go," Nicole said, as she placed the baskets in front of her siblings.

None of them moved until Jessica tapped her fingertips on the table. Two taps on the table and they looked up at the food. Each one of them picked up their portion of the burger and took a very small bite, before placing it back into the basket and putting their hands in their laps while they chewed.

Nicole's parents were bad when she lived in the house, but it had seemed as though they had become more controlling over the kids since she had moved out. She couldn't stand how miserable her siblings looked. All seven of them had sad looks on their faces.

"Why do they sit like that?" Nicole asked Jessica.

"What's wrong with the way they are sitting? They aren't running around like animals and they are being obedient," Jessica replied, with a condescending tone.

"Johnny, Jimmy and Joe are three. Most three year olds have energy. Also, Brittney is only five and Tiffany is seven. They should also have energy. None of them has moved faster than a snail. The three little ones seem as though they have been drugged. Brittney and Tiffany even seem lethargic. As for Monica and Erin, they seem terrified to do anything until you allow them to. What did you do to them?"

"I'm making sure that none of them turn out to be

like you. You are too opinionated and mouthy and I need them to be obedient. You will understand when you start having children someday. They are easier to control when they are obedient. Fear is fundamental in parenting."

"I'm glad to know that you think I am such a horrible child." Nicole turned and headed toward the back to join Armando and Melanie. Jessica was frustrating her so much, she didn't know how much longer she could wait to murder the bitch.

"Having fun out there with your mother?" Armando asked.

She smiled at her husband, then opened the door to the walk in freezer and stepped inside. Armando furrowed his brow and Melanie just stared at her confused. She closed the door and made sure it was sealed before she screamed as loud as her voice would allow.

Once she had released her frustration, she took a deep breath and opened the door. Stepping out of the freezer, both Armando and Melanie were standing next to each other, puzzled.

"What was that?" Melanie asked.

"My mother can be very condescending and she knows how to piss me off. I held my tongue this time and just walked away from her. She is inciting fear in my siblings and requiring them to be obedient. I still believe she may have drugged the three little ones, but I don't have any proof," Nicole explained.

"Well, we have about five minutes before we open, so let's finish setting up and prepare for the lunch crowd," Armando told his wife, wrapping his arms around her shoulders.

"You're right. Melanie, you want to help me finish setting up the cold bar and open the doors?" Nicole asked.

"Let's go," Melanie said, putting a little pep in her step.

Melanie was generally a positive person. There had been a few times a rude person had changed her mood, but she always tended to bounce back fairly quickly. That was the main reason Nicole enjoyed being around her.

Once everything was set and Armando was prepared for customers, Nicole stepped behind the counter and motioned for Melanie to open the doors. As soon as the doors opened, it seemed as though the entire town entered.

"Welcome to the Roadkill Café. You kill it, we grill it. How may I help you?" Nicole greeted the customers, as they flooded in and up to the counter to order.

Five

As each customer ordered, Nicole rang them up, took payment, then moved on to the next. She could hear the printer in the kitchen, spitting out the orders faster than Armando could keep up.

Nicole was so glad when Melanie realized that her husband was probably becoming overwhelmed and headed to the back to help him out. He ran the grill and she ran the fryer.

"Looks like your grand opening is successful, eh Nicole?" Bernard said, as she placed his order down in the pick-up area.

"I'm so glad everyone decided to give us a try. I just hope the food is good enough to keep y'all coming back," Nicole responded.

"If I can build my own burger, I'll come by everyday, hun. Keep being sweet," Bernard said, kissing the back of her hand, before taking his food and heading over to the cold bar.

"The build your own burger bar is going over amazingly with the locals. Thank you Melanie," Nicole said through the food window, as she picked up the next order.

"Whew, baby girl. Y'all are doing great. Keep it up," Betty told me.

"Thank you. Please enjoy your meal," Nicole told her.

"Make sure you stop by the shop next weekend. I'm getting a new shipment in and I'll give you the sale price on anything you buy. There are several outfits that I think would look cute on you," Betty said, as she picked up her food.

Nicole nodded. "I absolutely will. You always have the best recommendations."

Once all the orders had been delivered and everyone was enjoying their food, Nicole was finally able to take a deep breath and relax. She turned and peered in at Armando and Melanie cleaning up the kitchen area.

"Well, you were a little busy. Were you going to feed your father and I, or are we just supposed to stand around and watch everyone else eat?" Nicole's mother yelled across the restaurant at her.

Nicole let out a deep breath, stepped out from behind the order counter and approached the table where her parents were sitting. "I can take your order. Do you want one burger split in half, or do each of you get your own burger?"

"Nicole, really? You know your father and I can't get full on half a burger. Where is your brain?" Jessica said.

"You're right, I'm sorry. What was I thinking. Did

you want French fries, or onion rings?"

"Go ahead and do one of each, thank you."

The condescending tone in her mother's voice would have pissed Nicole off, but she clenched her teeth and fake smiled at Jessica. She turned around, walked back over behind the order counter and repeated the order to Armando. He reached into a different meat container, forming the burgers and placing them on the grill.

Melanie finished in the kitchen and came around to the front. She stepped up behind the counter with Nicole, as she wiped down the counter. Jessica was picking French fries out of the baskets from each of the triplet's food. They were the youngest and had been trained not to eat as much as the others.

"What's the deal with the separate meat containers? Armando had been making the burgers for the customers from the large container in the walk-in cooler, but when he went to make the burgers for your parents, he reached into the mini fridge and took the meat from a smaller container," Melanie asked.

For the first time since her parents had arrived,

Nicole flashed Melanie a genuine smile. "That is our special meat. Freshly scraped off the road and ground up."

Melanie giggled. "Oh, that's funny. If I hadn't of had an interaction with her earlier, this wouldn't be as satisfying to watch."

Armando placed the baskets up in the window and Nicole turned around. She picked the baskets up, then turned back and placed them in the customer pick-up area.

"Mom, your food is ready," she called out to Jessica.

"What? You're not going to do your job and bring it to us?" her mother snarked at her.

"There is a pick up area so you are able to put your own toppings on your burger," Marvin told her, in the most polite tone he could muster after watching Nicole's mother berate her.

"I'm sorry, but I didn't ask for your opinion. Please mind your own business. Nicole, bring it here," her mother demanded.

"Ma'am," Marvin started, but Nicole cut him off.

"It's okay, Marvin. That's my mother," she told him.

"It still doesn't give her the right to speak to you that way," Marvin said, with a slight tone of irritation in his voice that Nicole had never heard from him before.

She picked up her parents food and walked it over to where they were sitting. "I'm use to it," she told Marvin, as she dropped off the food.

Marvin went ahead and backed off. Nicole turned and walked back to the order counter, just as she heard Jessica's voice from behind her. "We only get plain burgers?"

"No, mom. There is a full service bar, right next to the pick-up area where you can dress your burger however you like," Nicole told her, smiling at Marvin.

Jessica scoffed. "I don't know how you can run a successful food service business if the customers are supposed to do everything themselves."

Nicole held her arms up over her head in order to get the attention of the other patrons in the establishment. "Does anyone here have a problem with building their own burger with toppings?"

Bernard stood. "I think it's awesome. That means I

can put whatever I want on my burger. More mayo, less mustard and a splash of ketchup. Extra onions and jalapeños. No lettuce or tomatoes."

Marvin stood after Bernard returned to his seat. "It makes it easier on Armando to only have to focus on cooking the food and not having to make sure that the toppings are correct for each individual order."

Betty chose to chime in as well, but she addressed Jessica directly. "You're a horrendously selfish woman. Your daughter is a remarkable young lady and everyone of us here in this little podunk town are absolutely proud of her and what she has accomplished. You're not better than anyone, so stop acting like you are."

Jessica sat with her mouth agape, shocked that strangers had defended a child. At that point, she was genuinely crying. She rested her arms on the table and grabbed her elbows, as she looked down at her lap; tears dripping onto her pants. Jerry stood up and walked over to the cold bar to put toppings on their burgers. Marvin smiled at Nicole, then the rest of the patrons went back to the conversations they were having with the rest of the locals around them.

Jerry went to the cold bar with each burger one at a time, so Jessica could stay with Nicole's siblings. She could tell that her mother felt humiliated. She never looked up, nor spoke to any of the other patrons. Melanie was staring at both Jerry and Jessica, with her head tilted to the side, as if she was trying to figure out why they were such horrible people.

"Why are you looking at my parents like that?" Nicole asked her.

"I'm trying to figure out how to save your siblings, so they can be children," she told Nicole.

"The only way to save them, would be to murder my parents," Nicole responded, laughing as though she were joking.

"If they stay for the day, it will only be a few more hours before we can take care of that," Melanie said, smirking.

Nicole sighed and nodded. "Hopefully what Betty said to her doesn't cause her to just leave."

"Do you think that maybe your mother would just brush it off as the ramblings of an elderly woman?"

"Not at all. My mother doesn't allow anyone to

speak to her like that. Since Betty is an elderly woman, that's why my mother didn't talk back to her. If I would have said what Betty said, my mother probably would have walked over here and slapped me across the face."

"Well then, soon she will be used as filler and you will save your siblings."

"We have to make sure to get rid of my father first. He has choked me to the point where I almost passed out. I know for a fact that if he finds out that we killed my mother, he will become violent with everyone involved. If he isn't compliant with her out in public, then she withholds sex from him. That is the only reason why he is so docile right now."

Melanie turned with her back to Nicole's family, but pointed over her shoulder. "Look, they are ruining those children. Your sister Tiffany has looked up at them a couple of times, which they hadn't noticed and had a look on her face as though one day she will murder them. You should at least save her from the trauma of killing her parents."

"When we finally do that, it would be to save all seven of them from the trauma of continuing to grow up in that house," Nicole said.

"Oh, absolutely. I made sure to put your parents in the room with a hidden door, so Bernard and Marvin have easy access to grab them straight out of the room," Melanie told her.

"I have an idea on how to get them over here and into the freezer. If that doesn't work out, then I will definitely appreciate the help from Bernard and Marvin. My problem is, what do I tell my siblings when they go to bed with mommy and daddy in the next motel room, but wake up and they are gone?" Nicole wondered.

"We will figure it out. I'm so ready for them to be eliminated," Melanie said, rubbing her hands together like a super villain.

Six

During the lunch service, several teens from town had been setting up games and fun stuff for the kids to do. Melanie, along with the rest of the town, wanted the grand opening to be successful and was hoping to attract anyone that just happen to be driving through town.

Nicole was surprised when Jessica allowed Tiffany, Brittney and the triplets to actually play. Johnny, Jimmy and Joe played in the bouncy house. Tiffany and Brittney had fun with the bean bag toss. Monica and Erin were, at first, forced to stand guard to make sure the triplets didn't get hurt and Brittney didn't throw a tantrum.

Tiffany and Brittney were always playing together, which kept Jessica happy because that meant she didn't have to watch her own children. Even though Tiffany was only seven, Nicole's mother felt as though it was old enough to take care of her five year old sister. The only issue was that Brittney could be a little bossy. If Brittney didn't get her way, she would throw a monster temper tantrum. That would get Tiffany in trouble and she would get beat with a belt.

Jessica and Jerry liked to turn the beatings into a group effort where Jerry would hold down whichever child was in trouble and Jessica would swing the belt. Monica always kept an eye on Brittney in order to keep Tiffany from getting into trouble for nothing. Eventually some of the locals had approached and encouraged

Monica and Erin to play volley ball in the side yard. Jessica rolled her eyes and huffed when she had to go over and keep an eye on the triplets herself.

Once the dinner rush was winding down and Melanie had offered to keep an eye on the register, Nicole went out to check on her family. Jessica was standing outside the opening of the bounce house with Tiffany quietly crying next to her and Brittney with a satisfied look on her face.

"Boys, please come out of there." Jessica was trying to coax them out.

"NO!" all three of them screeched.

Jessica grabbed Tiffany by her shirt and practically shoved her into the bounce house. "Tiffany, go get your brothers."

"How is everything going? Are the kids having fun?" Nicole asked her mother.

"Monica and Erin are absolutely useless. I can't believe they chose to go play with those kids, instead of keeping an eye on their siblings and forcing me to stand here because your baby brothers wanted to jump," Jessica complained.

Johnny, Jimmy and Joe screamed as Tiffany grabbed them one by one and forced them out of the bounce house. She sat in the opening, so they couldn't climb back in and Johnny bit her leg.

"Owe! Mom, he bit me," Tiffany cried.

"Johnny, don't bite your sister," Jessica said, stoically. "Stop crying, Tiffany. You're fine."

"Seriously? That's how you're going to handle his behavior?" Nicole said.

Jessica rolled her eyes and sighed heavily. "He's just a baby. She's fine. Tiffany is just being a little bitch."

Nicole knelt down in front of her brother and wagged her finger in his face. "Johnny, you don't bite your sister. That was wrong. Now apologize to Tiffany and don't do that again."

Johnny screamed loudly in Nicole's face and bawled uncontrollably. Jessica bent down and scooped him up, cuddling him in her arms. When Nicole stood up and faced her mother, Jessica slapped Nicole across the face. "How dare you yell at him. Don't you ever talk to him like that again."

Nicole stared at her in shock. The sound of the slap garnered the attention of everyone in the vicinity. Monica and Erin left the volley ball area and ran over to stand next to their mother. All four of the girls stood with their arms down by their sides and stared at their feet. Jimmy and Joe were running circles around Jessica as she cradled Johnny.

"I guess your party is starting to wind down. We are going to take the kids over to the motel and put them to bed," Jessica said.

The hue in the sky shifted to a pinkish orange and people began leaving due to the uncomfortable situation. As Johnny calmed down and stopped screeching, Nicole placed her hand on her mother's shoulder.

"Could you and dad come back once they are settled, so we can talk?" Nicole requested.

"I guess so," Jessica said, rolling her eyes and turning to leave. "Jerry! Let's go."

Nicole's father stood up from the table he had been sitting at the entire day, drinking beer with a few of the other locals. Jessica's actions throughout the day truly solidified Nicole's decision to use her for hamburger meat. The fact that her father did nothing and basically sat back and allowed Jessica to verbally abuse their children, showed that he was back to physically abusing them behind closed doors rather than right out in the open.

Melanie stepped up next to Nicole on the front patio once she was alone. "Okay Nicole, everything is cleaned and put away. When do we get to butcher your mother?"

"I asked for her and my father to come back over here once my siblings were in bed," Nicole explained to her. "I feel like Armando and I should do this alone. I don't want to drag you in as an accessory."

"I'm already invested in this. I just want to help you do it right," Melanie said, with the biggest grin on her face. "Plus, Bernard and Marvin will be here later to assist with the dismemberment."

"I need to know how the three of you all got into this," Nicole said, grabbing her arm, dragging her inside and taking her over to a table to sit down.

Melanie raised her eyebrows. "We can have story time later, but for now I just want to focus on your problem."

Just as Armando joined them out front, Nicole's parents returned. Melanie stood up and headed toward the door to leave. "Hey, Nicole. I'll see you later."

Jessica pursed her lips and glared at Melanie. "Yes. You should actually go. You have been here all day and haven't paid enough attention to your own business. How about you go over to the motel and make sure my children stay in their room."

Melanie saluted Jessica. "Yes, ma'am. No problem, ma'am. I'll do your parenting for you, ma'am."

Jessica scoffed, as Melanie turned and skipped out of the café. "That woman is rude."

"So, what do you want to talk about?" Jerry began, sounding irritated.

Armando joined Nicole at the table she was sitting at. She motioned for her parents to join them before she started. "I feel like since I left home our relationship has become contentious. You are my parents and I feel as though y'all don't respect me, or my life decisions."

"You are *our* child. You are suppose to respect *us*, we don't have to respect *you*. Also, you chose to leave our house and that was disrespectful." The words Jessica spoke were spit like venom.

"I never chose to leave, you kicked me out because you kept having kids and needed more room. So you needed the oldest to move out in order to rotate the new ones in. As well, you have to give respect, to get respect. That includes with your children," Nicole responded.

"You think *you* deserve respect?" Jerry said, as he stood in a threatening manner. "You have never shown your mother or me any kind of respect and have always acted like an entitled little bitch."

Armando stood, in order to defend his wife if her father decided to put his hands on her. Nicole flinched and covered her face when her father slammed his hand down on the table in front of her.

"You two are the worst excuses for parents," Armando said, as he stepped around the table in order to get closer to them.

"Are you threatening me?" Jerry asked, when Armando stepped up to get in his face.

Jerry stood at five foot ten inches and weighed

around four hundred pounds, whereas Armando was six foot one inch and three hundred pounds of pure muscle. Armando towered over Nicole's father and with a quick motion, he grasped Jerry around his neck. Jessica stood up and started screaming, slapping Armando on his arm.

Jessica's screams attracted Melanie, from where she was waiting outside. She chose to stay nearby just in case. Nicole stood up, as Melanie ran in and wrapped a rope around Jessica's neck from behind. She looped it around her hands three times and pulled the ends tight. Jessica was only five feet tall and around two hundred fifty pounds, whereas Melanie was about five foot seven inches and built like a linebacker. Jerry struggled with Armando, as Jessica grabbed at the rope around her neck.

Nicole turned and headed toward the back of the restaurant where the large, walk-in freezer was located. Melanie dragged Nicole's mother with the rope around her neck as Jessica kicked her legs and Armando was leading Jerry with his hands around his neck as Jerry grasped at Armando's fingers; both assailants brought the victims to the back and toward the freezer.

Armando shoved his wife's father into the freezer, causing him to fall back and hit his head on a metal rack at the back wall. Melanie dragged Jessica into the freezer and left her on the floor with the rope still around her neck. Nicole's parents were gasping for air when Nicole shut the door and slipped the metal peg, that hung from a chain, into the hole on the door handle, in order to lock them inside.

Nicole exhaled, loudly. "Now we need to get rid of their car." She stared, almost expressionless at Melanie and Armando.

"I'll take care of it," Melanie said, holding up the car keys she managed to finagle out of Jessica's pocket as they passed each other before the argument ensued. "I know the best spot and route where I won't be seen by any witnesses."

"Awesome. Make sure you don't leave behind fingerprints and push it off a cliff. Hopefully it will catch fire and completely incinerate," Nicole said.

"Nicole, I got this. Don't worry. By the way, Bernard and Marvin should be here soon as well."

Melanie skipped off out of the restaurant. Nicole turned toward Armando and took a deep breath.

"Are you still okay with this?" Armando asked, wrapping his arms around his wife's shoulders.

"Absolutely! These two people have tormented me my entire life and I don't want that to happen to my siblings," Nicole said, pushing away from him. "Are you having second thoughts?"

"No, not at all. I want to protect you, but I don't want you to regret getting rid of your parents."

"I will never regret eliminating my abusers and those that abuse my siblings."

"Speaking of which, what do we tell your siblings happened to your parents?"

"I will tell them we had an argument and they left. After that, I have no idea what happened to them."

"Do you think that Monica will believe that?" Armando asked.

Nicole shook her head. "No and eventually I will have to explain to her what happened, but I need to make sure she is happier without them, before I tell her. I want to make sure I can trust her to keep her mouth shut."

"Okay, so now what do we do about your parents? They are still alive in there."

They both looked at the freezer, as her parents were banging on the door. When the banging slowed and the lock pin began jumping against the force, Nicole rubbed her face with her hands.

"I think my father is throwing his body weight against the door. Hopefully they will have stopped banging on the door by the time Melanie gets back because they are too cold. By the way, lining the entire freezer in plastic was a nice touch."

Armando flashed Nicole a sly smile. "I did make sure to leave the cooling fans uncovered."

"Oh yeah, let me turn the temperature down in there so they freeze faster," Nicole said, turning toward the thermostat and lowering the temperature.

Armando and Nicole had been waiting for Melanie for over half an hour, when the front door to the café opened. It was Marvin.

"Hey, what's up?" Nicole said, when Armando and she made their way up to the front.

"Bernard is heading out to pick up Melanie. Are they giving you trouble?" Marvin said, pointing toward the back.

"They are still trying to get out, but I think they should tire out soon," Nicole told him.

"Well, there is one thing I'm concerned about. When your dad was drinking with some of the locals from the next town over, he was talking about the fact that he lets your mother beat the kids because he beats your mother," Marvin told Nicole. "Do you think he would beat your mother to death in there?"

"Oh shit," Nicole responded, with a slight giggle. "I guess that's one less thing that we will have to worry about if he kills her. Also, him saying that he only beats my mother is complete bullshit."

"I guess that's true. Hopefully they don't break down the door though. Do you think that your father would try to use your mother's body as a battering ram to try to get out?" Armando asked.

Nicole shrugged and smiled at her husband. "Okay, I'm going to go check on my siblings before Melanie and Bernard get back. You can't kill my parents until I get back." Nicole grabbed Armando's hand and gazed lovingly into his eyes, before heading out to the motel.

Nicole pressed her ear against the door once she had stepped up to the room and could hear Monica's voice. "Look, I'm in charge here because I'm the oldest. Mom and dad left, but they could be back in the morning. Maybe they are using this as a mini vacation."

Erin grunted. "No! Nicole should be in charge. I should go get her."

"We are suppose to be in bed. Just relax and we can deal with it in the morning," Monica told her.

"Fine, but stop trying to boss us around. Deal with the boys because they are babies and need to be taken care of. I can take care of myself," Erin said.

Nicole giggled at their conversation, then headed back across the street without disturbing them. The plan she had for them, she knew they would be happier once their parents were gone.

Seven

By the time Nicole opened the door to the café, Bernard pulled into the parking lot with Melanie in the passenger seat. Nicole waved at them and waited for Melanie to exit the vehicle. She bounced out as Bernard, being in his late fifties, carefully climbed out from behind the steering wheel.

"Thank goodness no one drives down that road after the sun goes down. I was able to drive out there and shove the car down the embankment without seeing anyone else," Melanie said, as she closed the passenger door and skipped up next to Nicole.

"That's true. I don't think I have seen anyone drive past here since the sun set," Nicole told her, as the three of them walked into the café.

"No witnesses," Melanie said, giggling. "So how is this going to go?"

Nicole sat down at one of the tables and motioned for Melanie to join her. "For now, they are freezing. How about you tell me about the three of you and how y'all got involved in this kind of business."

Bernard sat down next to Melanie. "Okay, but you have to understand that none of us are psychopaths. Technically we are saving the general public from having to come into contact with these horrible, hateful people."

"I agree. I'm trying to save my siblings from a tortured childhood with my abusive parents," Nicole said, reaching across the table and touching his hand.

"I want to be included in this conversation," Marvin said, as he joined them in the dining area of the restaurant with Armando right behind him.

Armando walked over and sat down next to his wife, as Marvin settled on the side of the table with Bernard and Melanie. Melanie took a deep breath and shifted in her seat uncomfortably.

"So, you know how the motel has forty rooms, right?" Melanie began.

"Yeah," Nicole responded.

Melanie smiled. "Room one is reserved for rude people. If a tourist drives into town and is rude to anyone, I am notified by the local who came into contact with that person. I am sent a photograph, so if that person comes to check in to the motel, I put them in room one."

Armando furrowed his eyebrows. "What's in room one? And what happens if there is more than one rude person that comes to town and needs lodging?"

Bernard sat up straighter and spoke matter-of-factly. "Room one is the only room with an access door from the attached office. There is also a hidden camera so

Melanie can watch for when the guest goes to sleep. Once they are asleep, Marvin and I are able to sneak in with a knife and slit their throat.

"If more than one shows up, then I review the information that is sent to me and make the executive decision as to who goes into room one and is fucked up by Martin and Bernard. The other is placed in the last room and I go right in the front door an hour after the lights go out and stab them in the neck."

"Once that is done, what do you do with the dead bodies?" Nicole asked, with genuine curiosity.

Marvin decided to chime in. "When Gary owned this café, Bernard and I would wrap up the body then bring it over for Gary to use as filler."

"What have you been doing with the bodies since the café has been empty?" Armando asked.

Bernard smiled. "Well, I own a wood chipper. After we wrapped up the body, we would take it over to the General Store, hang it up in what is labeled as a store room out back and drain the blood from the body before taking it over to my shop and tossing it into the wood chipper. Melanie has always been in charge of getting rid of the vehicles, just like she did with your parents vehicle and that's it."

As Nicole took in the information, she picked at the skin on her fingers. Melanie, Bernard and Marvin were such sweet people. Nicole had no idea how they could cheerfully treat other people, no matter how horrible those other people were, as though they were just live-stock. However, she did feel better that she was working with professionals and that her parents would turn out to be exactly what they are…shit.

"Are you still okay with this?" Armando asked me.

"Getting rid of my parents? Absolutely. My mother has been nothing but sour since she arrived. Her being rude to me and my siblings is normal, but for her to be straight up hateful to everyone here in town is just gross." Nicole stood up and placed her hand on Armando's shoulder.

Melanie smiled and stood. "Okay. So once we finish with your parents, would you want to continue with other hateful people? We can kill them and transport the body over here, then you can grind them up into hamburger meat."

Bernard reached toward Nicole across the table. "Let's just get through the situation we are in right now. If you choose to continue after this, then we will come up with a plan that works for you."

Nicole leaned down and touched his hand. "Great! Let's go back there and butcher these assholes."

All five of them headed to the back of the café. As they stood outside of the freezer, we could hear Jerry yelling at Jessica.

"We are in this situation because you are a fucking bitch! You couldn't even go a single weekend without being a bitch to everyone around you! Before we left the house you were whining about the fact that the child you were disappointed in the most has chosen to stop talking to you and instead of trying to fix it, you decided to criticize her and the other hillbillies in this shitty little town! Maybe you should stop being such a bitch!" Jerry's deep voice bellowed from behind the big metal door.

The sound of Jessica sobbing could also be heard. "I just want my children to do what I tell them. I don't want them to be independent. I need to be needed and they have to show me that they need me, or I don't want them around. Both Nicole and Erin have been mouthy little bitches their entire lives and don't want me to do things for them. Since Nicole wanted to be independent, I shoved her out. I thought she would realize how hard life really is and she would come back to me."

The loud bang that came from the other side of the big metal door was most likely when Jerry punched the freezer door. "Well that shit backfired. All that did was force her into the arms of another man. She hates me because of you and how you have badmouthed me, but our children also don't have any relationships with other family members because of you. You have put your issues onto our children. Just because you can't control your sister or your parents, you have decided they are bad people. Get over yourself."

The yelling ceased and all we could assume was that Jerry was throwing things around in the freezer. Armando had removed any food from the freezer, but left the metal shelves. They figured he was just making a mess in there and they waited for him to tire himself out.

Once the banging stopped and they could be sure that neither one of them would try to escape, Armando opened the freezer door. Jessica laid on the floor of the freezer in the fetal position. Her face was swollen and bleeding. She was still breathing, but it was short, shallow breaths. Jerry was slumped in the corner. He was breathing heavily and his hands were covered in blood. Nicole wasn't sure if any of the blood belonged to him, or if it was all from Jessica.

"Well, here's something we never accounted for," Armando said.

Nicole shrugged her shoulders. "I figured he would beat on her a little, but I didn't think it would be that bad. She's already basically dead. Due to his medical issues, it could take him a couple of hours to catch his breath and be strong enough to fight back."

"We should probably start this now then. We should at least bleed the bodies before we remove the limbs," Bernard said, peeking in at Nicole's parents.

"You're right. We need to get this taken care of now that they are subdued. The freezer guy had mentioned adding metal rings in the ceiling just incase we had any fresh meat to hang up. I feel like this is the best time to figure out how much weight they will hold," Armando said, shrugging.

"Well, I guess since they have already worn themselves out, it will make this easier," Marvin said, turning and grabbing some rope from a shelf next to the freezer, along with two knives off the counter behind me.

Armando tied the rope that Marvin handed him to Jerry's ankles, then looped the other end through the metal ring in the ceiling of the freezer. Bernard helped as they pulled Jerry upside down and tied off the rope. The rope that Melanie had wrapped around Jessica's neck to get her into the freezer was conveniently laying at her feet.

Armando strung up Jessica the same as he had Jerry, as Bernard placed a couple of buckets directly below the two of them. Marvin handed one knife to Nicole and one knife to Armando. Melanie, Bernard and Marvin stood in the doorway to the freezer, as Armando and Nicole stepped inside. Nicole stood behind Jessica's hanging body and Armando stood behind Jerry.

Jessica was unconscious and Nicole wasn't sure if she was even still alive. She didn't squirm or move in any way. Jerry on the other hand was flopping around like a fish out of water and spouting profanities at Armando. We all chose to not respond to Jerry, but Bernard chose to enter the freezer and hold his dangling body still. Nicole grabbed a handful of her mother's hair and pulled her head back.

"What are you going to do?" Jessica asked, as she reached up and grabbed her daughter's wrist.

Nicole flinched due to the surprise of her touch. "I plan to eliminate a lifelong problem I've been having and assuring my siblings will be able to live a happier existence."

Nicole made sure to stand strong and continue with the plan as she placed the blade against her mother's throat. Jessica pleaded for her life, but Nicole wasn't listening to her. Nicole took a deep breath, closed her eyes and when she opened them, she sliced the knife across Jessica's neck, from ear to ear. Making sure to apply enough pressure to slice through the esophagus, she also made sure to place the knife over the carotid artery.

Most of the blood that poured from the wound, drained into the bucket that was placed below her. Once Jessica was gurgling on her own blood, Nicole let go of her hair and she just dangled from the ceiling of the freezer. Jerry was doing everything he could, struggling to get out of the hold that Bernard had around his body. Armando made one swift motion and sliced opened Jerry's throat, in almost the same way Nicole had done to her mother, but due to her father's short hair, Armando placed his hand on my father's forehead.

"They aren't going to hurt anyone, anymore," Nicole said, as Bernard stepped out of the freezer and Armando and Nicole stood behind the dangling bodies of her parents.

"What do we do with them now?" Melanie asked, rubbing her hands together.

"Nicole?" the sound of Erin's voice came from the front of the restaurant.

"Shit! Close the door," Nicole said, rushing Armando out of the freezer, so her sister wouldn't see what they had just done.

"Nicole?" Erin called again.

"Yeah, uh, back here," Nicole said, grabbing the knife from Armando and tossing both knives into a sink.

"Hey, do you know where mom and dad are?" Erin asked.

Nicole ran up to the dining area, so she wouldn't come to the back. "No. I would have assumed that after I pissed them off, they would have gone back over to the motel. Are they not in their room?"

"The car is gone. A while ago, Monica thought she saw the headlights come on and the car leave, but she wasn't sure if it was them. When she looked out the window, she said mom's car was gone. I told her that we should tell you, but she just wanted to boss us around and told us to go to bed," Erin explained.

Nicole furrowed her eyebrows. "If she told you to go to bed, how are you here now?"

Erin looked down at her bare feet. "When Monica fell asleep, I snuck out. I just wanted to know if you saw the car leave, or if you knew where mom and dad went."

"I saw the car leave shortly after they stormed out of here," Nicole lied. "But I assumed they packed all you kids into the car and left because mom was mad at me."

"Mom is always mad at you," Erin said, rolling her eyes.

"I'm going to finish cleaning up here and I'll come over to check on y'all in a few minutes," Nicole told her sister, embracing her.

"Can I stay and help?" Erin asked.

Melanie joined us from the back. "We have a lot of sharp knives and things that could hurt you. I'm here to help, so it shouldn't take your sister too long."

Erin furrowed her eyebrows at Melanie, before she backed away from Nicole and headed back over to the motel. Nicole stood in the doorway and watched her run back over to the motel, before closing and locking the door. She wanted to make sure that none of her other siblings would walk in as they were dismembering the bodies of their parents.

"I don't think your sister likes me," Melanie said, as

they headed to the back of the café.

"It takes a little while for her to warm up to people. Plus, the shit that my mother says about people sinks in until the kids realize that she's a liar and a hateful bitch," Nicole told her, as Armando reopened the door to the freezer.

"Thank goodness I had them install that floor drain. It will be so much easier to clean up all this blood," Armando said, standing next to his wife, as they glared into the freezer.

Not only were the buckets under Jessica and Jerry filled with blood, there were a few places where there was cast off and arterial spray. It was a huge mess, but before they cleaned up, they needed to dismember the bodies and cut the meat off the bones. Luckily, the plastic contained most of the blood, so once they got that taken down, the mess left behind under it, wasn't so bad.

"So how is this going to work?" Nicole asked Bernard and Marvin.

"Well first, we need to cut down the bodies into easier to manage pieces. As a matter of fact, we could cut up the bodies tonight. Since they have been drained of blood, the pieces can be placed in containers and left inside the freezer. It will keep it fresh for now. In the morning you can just pull it out and grind it up as needed and we won't have to worry about whether or not your siblings will interrupt us again," Bernard explained.

"Sounds good to me. Let's chop these fuckers up," Nicole said, picking up a meat cleaver and heading into the freezer to get started.

Eight

Dismembering a body was a lot more difficult than Nicole thought. Bernard mentioned to start at the joints, which made it easier, but it was still a lot of work. Luckily, Armando was strong enough to pull the limbs and dislocate the joints. Melanie and Nicole wiped out the entire freezer, in order to clean up all the blood contamination.

Bernard, Marvin and Armando cut the meat off the bones, as Melanie and Nicole placed the pieces into plastic containers for storage. The two of them made sure to stick the date labels on the containers in order to be in compliance with the health department before putting them on the freezer shelves. Although, the health department would be the least of their worries. Marvin wrapped both Jessica and Jerry's heads in plastic and placed them on an empty shelf, to ensure safe storage. Bernard helped Melanie and Nicole dispose of the plastic that was lining the freezer.

Once they had shoved the plastic into the large kitchen trash can, Melanie and Nicole walked to the front of the café to get out of the way. Armando and Marvin were cleaning the floor and everything else in the kitchen area.

"Should the skin be flayed off the pieces before they are ground up?" Armando asked, as he tossed a water bucket on the floor of the kitchen area and squeegeed it down the drain.

Bernard had walked around to the front and was

leaning against the counter between the kitchen and the order area. "Gary always did because the skin can create a different flavor."

"What would be the best way to do that?" Armando asked.

"First, you will want to defrost the meat. It won't take very long. You will then need to wash it. Once it is washed, the skin should be just as easily flayed as a fish. As long as the meat pieces fit into the grinder, you should be able to grind it up into hamburger meat and serve. Of course, you are going to want to mix it in with your beef shipment so it lasts longer and you won't have to spend as much for each order," Marvin explained.

"Absolutely morbid. I love it!" Melanie said, rubbing her hands together like a super villain.

"What do we do with the bones?" Armando wanted to know.

Bernard patted his hand against the counter. "Oh, that's easy. Gary had built a fire pit out back. Bones will not burn to ash, but the fire will burn off the bone marrow and make them brittle. That means you can smash them down to smaller pieces and it will just look like animal bone pieces."

"I'm going to go check on my siblings and make sure they are okay," Nicole said, standing up from the table she was sitting at with Melanie and heading toward the exit.

Armando and Marvin made their way up to the dining area as they had finished cleaning and Melanie flicked her wrists, showing Nicole both her thumbs. Nicole headed out of the restaurant and across the street to the motel. Monica was standing in the open doorway of the kids room.

"Where is mom and dad?" Monica yelled at me, as Nicole approached.

"I don't know, but I came over to check to see if they had returned," Nicole lied.

"No, they abandoned us here and we have no way to get home. Why the hell would they just leave us here?" Monica complained, turning around and heading into the room.

Tiffany, Brittney and the triplets were still awake. The triplets and Brittney were on their knees, bouncing on one of the two double beds. Erin and Tiffany sat on the other bed with their legs dangling off the side. Monica stood next to Nicole at the foot of the bed Erin and Tiffany sat on.

"Why aren't any of you asleep?" Nicole wanted to know.

"Mom and dad aren't around, so we were taking the time to be independent," Erin said.

"Independent?" the eldest sister wondered.

"Mom and dad don't allow us to do anything we want to do. We are only allowed to obey their commands and we are relieved they left. Until they return, we are going to have fun and be real kids," Erin said, bouncing on the bed on her knees just like the youngest kids.

"Erin, this isn't funny. Mom and dad are missing. Who is supposed to take care of us now?" Monica said, as she walked over and sat in the chair in the corner of the room.

Erin bounced off the bed and landed on her feet. She walked over and stood in front of Monica. "When the hell have mom and dad ever taken care of us? They are so selfish and only care about themselves. Even Nicole has taken care of us better than our parents ever have when we were Brittney and the triplet's age."

Nicole sat down on the corner of the bed that was closest to where Monica was sitting. "Look, maybe they just went for a drive and they will be back soon. One thing I can't figure out is why you are so worried about them."

"They are the ones who pay the bills at the house," Monica said, rubbing her hands through her hair.

"But it's your money they are using to pay those bills. Technically, you're paying the bills," Nicole assured her.

"What if they finally decided they hated us and found an opening to abandon us with you?" Monica said, beginning to rock back and forth in her chair.

Nicole slid off the bed, knelt down in front of Monica and placed her hands on Monica's knees. "Mom and dad don't hate y'all."

"Bullshit, Nicole! If they actually cared for us, you wouldn't have been kicked out of the house and we would be fed on a regular basis. We wouldn't be slapped in the face for not knowing the answer on our homework. Did you know that we aren't allowed to look at anyone in the face? If we make eye contact with anyone, including them, dad makes us pull our pants down to expose our bare ass and he spanks us in front of everyone who just happens to be in the room; one time for each year of our age. Can you imagine how humiliating that is?" Monica told her sister, as she began to breathe heavily.

"Monica, you need to calm down. I will take care of all of you until mom and dad return," Nicole told her, just to ease her sister's anxiety.

"What if they never come back? That would be awesome," Erin said, climbing back up onto the bed and proceeding to bounce on her knees, with a smile on her face.

"Erin, stop jumping on the bed. Jimmy, Joe, Brittney and Johnny, y'all need to lay down and go to sleep. Nicole, we will see you in the morning and hopefully mom and dad will be back by then," Monica said, standing and rubbing her face.

"You're not in charge, Monica. For once, can we

just be kids?" Tiffany said, as she decided to join in with the others and bounce on the bed.

"Well, someone has to be in charge with mom and dad gone. Do what I tell you," Monica chastised.

"Monica, relax. You don't like it when mom and dad treat you that way, so don't act like mom," Nicole criticized her.

"Fuck off, Nicole!" Monica yelled. "Never say that I act like mom!"

"Then stop telling us what to do and enjoy the free time," Erin said, standing on the bed and jumping up and down.

Tiffany, Brittney and the triplets all stood up on their bed and joined in with Erin as she jumped up and down. Monica took a deep breath before heading out of the room.

"Okay, you six, stop jumping on the beds before you hurt yourselves. I'm going to check on Monica," Nicole told them.

They each bounced down on their beds onto their bottoms, as they giggled. Nicole was just glad they were smiling and having fun. The eldest sister left the door to the motel room open, as she stepped out to join her sister.

"Monica, please. With mom and dad gone, you can finally be who you want to be and not who they want you to be. Embrace yourself," Nicole told her, rubbing her back.

She shrugged off my touch and turned to face me. "Nicole, you don't understand how them leaving us could completely disrupt our entire lives."

"Explain to me how this could disrupt your lives, rather than make it better."

"Once someone notices we didn't come home, they could call the police and report us all missing. Once the cops realize we are here and they are not, the four of us that still live in the home will be separated and shipped off to different foster homes. Tiffany, Brittney, Jimmy, Joe and Johnny will not be able to deal with being separated from the rest of us. Especially the triplets. They're just toddlers and haven't started school yet. Tiffany may be okay because she's older and could potentially thrive without us, but our brothers don't know how to interact with other people."

"What if in the morning, if they haven't come back, I call and report them missing. That way, when they see y'all are with me, maybe y'all will be able to stay here."

"I guess we will find out in the morning. For your sake, I hope they come back."

"What do you mean by that?"

"You just started your adult life. You shouldn't have to be in charge of someone else's children."

"Can you just relax and enjoy the time you have without mom and dad for now?" Nicole asked Monica.

"Fine, but if we never see you again after tomorrow morning, I'm blaming you for mom and dad leaving us," Monica said, touching the tip of her finger to the tip of Nicole's nose.

Nicole grabbed ahold of her and wrapped her arms around her shoulders, embracing her sister. "I'll take it."

Nine

The next morning, Armando and Nicole unintentionally slept in. Nicole was awoken to the sound of someone knocking on the door to the cabin they lived in behind the café. She checked the clock before she gently kissed her husband on his cheek. He roused awake, then she stepped out of the cabin to find out who wanted their attention.

When Nicole had opened the door, Monica was pacing back and forth in front of the cabin. "Hey, girl. What's going on?"

"They never came back last night and still aren't back. If you are sure that we can all stay together if you are the one to report them missing, better sooner rather than later," Monica told her.

Nicole yawned and rubbed her face. "What if I called grandma first? Maybe the triplets and Brittney can go with her."

Monica shook her head. "No. Mom never let us get to know our grandparents and she has always bad mouthed everyone on her side of the family, the little ones would never go with grandma."

"Where are the other kids?" Nicole asked.

"I told them to stay in the room."

"Go get them. The police may want to talk to them."

Monica scoffed and rolled her eyes as she turned to head back to the motel. Nicole reentered the cabin to dress for the day. Armando was just getting out of the shower and he was patting a towel along his body. She watched him for a few moments, imagining rubbing her hands over his skin.

Nicole had to snap out of her fantasy and prepare her story in order to report her parents missing. Her siblings couldn't know what happened to them and she needed to make sure that she was convincing. Since Monica believed that their parents had just left and never returned, Nicole was hoping the police would believe it as well. However, she wasn't going to report them missing until the end of the week. She just needed to convince her siblings that the police wouldn't do anything until then. If they could just feel the freedom of being without their parents and be happy kids, maybe they could just forget about the situation and enjoy their lives.

As soon as both Armando and Nicole were dressed, they headed out to meet up with her siblings. The seven of them were sitting on a bench just outside the front door of the café.

"Are the police coming?" Monica asked, standing as Armando and Nicole approached them.

"The police won't make a report until they have been missing for at least seventy two hours, so we will have to wait it out for another three days," Armando said, trying to help out his wife with them.

Nicole wasn't sure if that was true, but she was hoping the information would help Monica relax some. At that point, she decided to do everything she could to make sure that her siblings were able to salvage some semblance of a childhood for at least the next few days.

"Fine, but what do we do until then? We can't stay in the motel forever," Monica said.

"Let's just have fun for a few days and we can figure that out later," Erin told Monica. "I hope they never come back and we can just stay here."

"I'm sure that Melanie will allow y'all to stay for as long as you need to. Plus, I know the town construction contractor. Armando and I can have extra rooms added onto our cabin for y'all as well, if you end up staying with us," Nicole told them.

"That would be awesome. Nicole is so much more fun than mom and dad have ever been," Tiffany said.

"How do you know? You were too young to remember too much about Nicole before she was kicked out of the house," Monica said, playfully nudging her younger sister.

"I remember times that mom and dad would force her to babysit, so they could leave the house," Tiffany replied.

"Whatever. So what do we do for the next three days? I'm not going to babysit Tiffany, Brittney and the triplets," Monica said, crossing her arms over her chest.

"I don't expect you to. If you would like, Armando and I would like you to work in the café. Since our opening day was so successful, we should probably hire a helper. You could work at the front counter and take orders," Nicole suggested.

"Would I get paid, or is it like the babysitting situation with mom?" Monica asked, rolling her eyes.

"We would pay you. You would be an employee. What is the babysitting situation with mom?" Nicole inquired.

"She says since they are my siblings, I shouldn't expect to get paid to be with family," Monica told her, straightening her arms by her sides and balling up her fists.

"While you are working in the café, you are an employee. After you clock out and are no longer working, then you are family. That means you shouldn't expect preferential treatment while you are on the clock, just because you are my sister," Nicole reassured her.

"Okay, but what happens if the police decide we can't stay here with you?" Monica wondered, relaxing her stance.

"That's why we need to make sure y'all are being taken care of before we are able to report them missing. That way, the police will allow y'all to stay. It wouldn't be fair to separate the eight of us," Nicole told Monica.

"What about me?" Erin asked.

"What do you want to do?" Nicole asked her.

"Can I work in the café too?" Erin wanted to know.

"You are only fifteen. I can't put you on a business payroll. What I can do though, is offer you a little pay to watch Tiffany and Brittney a couple nights each week," Nicole told her.

"Like twenty dollars each time?" Erin asked, smiling and bouncing on her toes.

"I can give you twenty dollars, if that's what you want," Nicole said.

Erin skipped around the parking lot. "Awesome, I'll do it."

"Okay Monica, you never have to watch your siblings again. Now you get to be your own person. You have a job and can spend your money however you want," Nicole told her.

"And now I'm going to skip around the parking lot with Erin," Monica said, joining Erin.

"What about us?" Tiffany asked, holding Brittney's hand with the triplets standing in front of them.

"For right now, I just need the five of you to have fun and be kids. Can y'all do that for me?" Nicole asked, bending over and placing her hands on her knees.

Tiffany and Brittney exchanged a look, before giggling and running off to go play with Erin and Monica in the parking lot. As her siblings danced and skipped around, it was the first time since they had arrived, that they were actually smiling and laughing.

After a few moments, Melanie came walking over

from the motel. Armando went inside the café to get started on grinding up the pieces of Jessica and Jerry and Nicole sat down on the bench watching as Melanie danced with her siblings before joining her.

"This is the first time I have seen them actually being children," Melanie said, as she sat down on the bench with Nicole.

"Isn't it great? When my parents aren't around, they are actually great kids. It's mostly my mother's influence. My dad travels for work and is hardly ever home, but my mother is always there. She's the one who has always bad mouthed other family members, so we don't have a relationship with our aunt, or grandparents on her side of the family. She has always said that they are horrible people, but I had never experienced them being horrible ever. As for my dad, all of his family lives in a different state and we have never met any of them," Nicole explained.

"Why not reach out to them now?" Melanie asked.

"Well, my aunt decided she could no longer deal with my mother's narcissistic personality, so I haven't seen or heard from her since before my brothers were born. As for my grandparents, when my mother became pregnant with the triplets, she didn't tell them she was pregnant. She had a baby shower and everything without telling them about baby numbers six, seven and eight. Their birthday is December sixteenth.

"When my parents showed up for Christmas that year with several new babies, my grandparents were pissed that she wouldn't share that information with them," Nicole continued.

"Why didn't your mother tell her own parents that she was pregnant again?" Melanie wondered.

"It's most likely because she can't take a joke. My grandparents and aunt would make jokes every time she had another girl."

"But babies number six, seven and eight were finally boys. Why didn't she want to share that news?"

"Technically, I believe that my mother hated her family because they couldn't be manipulated by her. In turn, she just kept having kids because she realized how easy it was to manipulate her own children. We did everything she said because if we didn't, we were beaten. Either by her weapon of choice, or my father would slam us against the wall before screaming in our face."

"I'm surprised you're as strong as you are. Growing up in a home like that must have been hard."

"Erin has been counting down the years until she gets to move out because she wants out of that house so bad. She overheard my mother talking to someone on the phone a couple of years ago and she was crying and complaining that she didn't want to keep Erin because she was girl number three. My mother hated her from the moment she found out she was having another girl. The worst part about that, is Erin has known basically her entire life that our mother hated her. I'm so glad we were able to save them from the horrible life they were living," Nicole concluded.

"Well, it makes me happy knowing that the two people I helped you dismember are total duche bags," Melanie said.

"This incident isn't going to change the way the locals see us, is it?"

"This town has different kinds of people living here. We each take part in eliminating shitty people. It's natural selection and population control. In other words, y'all fit in perfectly here."

"Awesome. Now I need to find something to do with the kids while the grown-ups are working," Nicole said, laughing.

Ten

Melanie told Nicole about Ashley who ran an in home childcare and was willing to watch the five little ones while Armando, Monica and Nicole were working at the café. Erin was able to stay in the motel room alone. Nicole didn't want to put the responsibility of having to watch someone else's children onto a fifteen year old. The town also had a homeschool group that met up three times a week in an old schoolhouse that held about forty kids and Erin would be going there during the week.

Nicole made sure Erin was comfortable before she left her to hang out in the motel room by herself. Monica took Tiffany, Brittney and the triplets over to the motel office to call the town childcare provider, Ashley. She told Nicole that Ashley had a van and she would be willing to pick up the kids.

Monica and Nicole waited in the parking lot of the motel for Ashley to arrive. "Are you sure this woman is trustworthy to take care of Tiffany, Brittney and the triplets?"

Nicole rolled her eyes and sighed. "Come on. I have met mostly everyone in this town and haven't found a single person who is as bad as mom was."

"So who is Ashley? Other than the fact that she runs the daycare," Monica asked.

Melanie stepped out of the motel office and joined them. "Ashley is Betty's daughter. Betty owns the boutique in town. She's the sweet old lady that shut your mother down yesterday when she was being a total bitch."

Before Monica could respond, Ashley pulled up in the daycare van. Melanie walked up to the driver's window to speak with Ashley, as Monica gathered Tiffany, Brittney and the triplets. The youngest siblings latched onto her, as Nicole opened the side sliding door to the van.

"Thank you, Ashley. I really appreciate your help," Nicole told her.

"I think your sister needs some help," Ashley said, pointing at Monica who was wrestling with the other five to get them to the van.

Nicole rubbed her face with her hands, then mustered her scariest mom voice and snapped her fingers. "Tiffany and Brittney! Get into the van. Stop right now. Johnny, Jimmy and Joe! That's enough! Get in the vehicle!"

The five little ones let go of Monica and climbed into the vehicle. Tiffany helped the triplets into the booster seats that had been provided and buckled their seatbelts before she sat down in the row of seats behind them, next to Brittney and buckled her own seatbelt. They all cried quietly.

Nicole leaned into the van and snapped her fingers at her siblings to get their attention. "I know mom lets you be disrespectful to everyone, but if I find out that the five of you were rude to Mrs. Ashley, I will make you clean the entire café after dinner service. All of you better be nice."

All five of them nodded and Nicole closed the side sliding door. Melanie backed away from the van and waved as Ashley drove out of the parking lot. Monica stood with her head down and her hands down in front of her with her fingers intertwined.

Melanie patted her on her shoulder. "They will be just fine. Ashley may not have any kids, but she has taken several parenting classes, she has a major in early childhood development, as well as being CPR and first aid certified."

Monica sighed. "They can be a lot to handle. Tiffany and Brittney say rude things that makes you want to slam their faces into a table and the triplets just cry if they don't get what they want, when they want it.

My mother has never required the boys to speak so they don't exactly know how to use their words. They will just scream and cry. I just hope that since my mother didn't get the chance to badmouth Ashley, they will come to their own conclusion as to who she is as a person before they act like the assholes that my mother allows them to be."

Nicole walked over to her sister as Melanie walked toward the motel office, laughing. "From what Melanie told me, Ashley has worked with difficult kids before. Hopefully she can change them into being good kids. Hell, most of the time I don't want to be around any of them because mom has basically raised them to be feral children and they just do whatever they want."

Monica took a deep breath. "Okay, let's go get started at the café, so you can teach me how to do whatever it is that you want me to do."

Nicole draped one arm across her shoulders and led her across the street to the restaurant. They entered through the front door and heard the water running from the kitchen area. Nicole knew that was Armando washing pieces of her parents to flay the skin before grinding them up. Not wanting her sister to see what her husband was doing, she took her behind the order counter.

"Okay, Monica. I'm going to teach you how to use the register system," Nicole told her sister.

"Awesome! You're going to let me run the register?" Monica said.

"Absolutely. All you have to do is is push the button that corresponds with what the customer orders. If they order a drink, just press the button that says fountain. There are cups next to the drink machine and the customers are welcome to help themselves.

"The menu is simple. We have hamburgers and they can choose between French fries, or onion rings. The burgers are plain, or they can add cheese. Once you press burger, it's either kids, junior, or large. Then you have the option for no cheese, or make a selection from the cheese list.

"When the customer decides on their side, the amount is determined by the size of the burger they chose. There is a bar to set up all the fixin's for the burgers and the customer can dress up their burger however they want," Nicole explained. "Do you have any questions?"

"So how does the kitchen get the order? Do I pass the order to Armando?" Monica asked.

"No. As soon as the customer pays, a ticket is printed in the kitchen with the order on it. Armando will make the order, plate it up, then place it on the bar behind you with the ticket that printed out, so you know who the order goes to."

"How do I know which order goes to who?"

"When you get to the pay screen, the register will populate a customer number. Make sure to give the customer their receipt with the order number on it and it will print on the ticket that prints in the kitchen. That way, when Armando places the order up on the bar with the ticket, the number on the ticket will correspond with the number the customer was given on their receipt."

"Okay, that seems easy. So if I take over the register, what will you be doing?"

"I will make sure all supplies are stocked. Like the cups, the burger toppings bar, napkins and when we are busy, you ring up the orders and I will call them out. We open in fifteen minutes. Are you ready for this?" Nicole asked, glaring at the overwhelmed look on Monica's face.

"I think I could pick it up as I go along. It doesn't seem that hard," Monica said, staring at the register screen in front of her and taking a deep breath.

"Good. I will stay with you for the first few orders just to make sure you get it before I leave you to do it by yourself. Now I'm going to prep the toppings bar and make sure everything is ready for when we open."

Nicole patted Monica on her shoulder and left her to get comfortable with the order area. As she stepped around to the back, Armando had placed all of the prepped veggies and condiments onto a wheelie cart. He smiled as his wife leaned in for a kiss, before she pushed the cart out to the front area.

Monica was wiping down the tables, as Nicole stocked the cold bar. Armando had been working all morning, grinding up Jessica and Jerry into hamburger meat. As Monica and Nicole prepared the seating area to receive customers, Armando was preparing the meat into different sized hamburger patties.

Once they were ready and Nicole had returned the cart back to the kitchen, she unlocked the front doors and stood behind the order counter with Monica. The entire town filed in on day two and Nicole began bouncing on her toes with a wide grin on her face.

"Welcome to the Roadkill Café. You kill it, we grill it," Nicole greeted the customers, as they stepped up to order.

Monica was slow at first, but eventually found her groove and was able to get the customers rung up and paid out within three minutes. Nicole had to leave her a few times to refill the cold bar with toppings and condiments, but Monica did well without her sister. As the line fizzled off and the last customer received their food, Melanie came in and rushed up to the counter.

"I just checked in the biggest hoity toity bitch," Melanie said, slamming her hand on the counter.

"I think that might be the same bitch who came into the general store this morning. She told me my store was gross and we all look like hill-billies," the owner of the general store, George, piped in to the conversation.

"Is she alone?" Bernard asked.

"She checked in alone and went into her room alone, so I assume she is alone," Melanie said.

"Are we going to take care of her?" George asked, directed toward me.

"Can we talk about this later?" Nicole said, tipping my head toward Monica.

"Oh, yeah. No problem," Bernard said, touching the side of his nose with his first finger.

"What are they talking about?" Monica asked.

"Poisoning," Nicole told her, shrugging and laughing, pretending to make a joke. "How about you go check the inventory and make sure we still have enough fixin's. Armando will direct you in the kitchen."

Monica knew Nicole was trying to get rid of her, so she rolled her eyes and walked away. Once she was out of earshot, Bernard, Marvin and George pulled a couple of chairs up to the front counter.

"So I'm guessing y'all told George about my parents?" Nicole asked Bernard and Marvin.

"Of course we did. Remember when we said that we use to take the bodies to the shed behind the general store? George was there. Now, we can all work together with the disposal," Bernard said, grinning.

"I know Melanie said that Bernard would toss them in the wood chipper, but what about George? George, other than your shed behind the store, how do you help with the disposal?" Nicole wanted to know.

"I drive the truck with the tarp covering what is in the back. All I have to do is back the truck up to the door of the motel room and slide the body into the bed of my truck. I was driving it over to the general store so we could drain the bodies of blood and dismember each one into easily choppable pieces so Bernard could toss it into the wood chipper," George said.

"If that's how it was done before, how do I fit into this? I feel like I'm ruining the flow of the town's population control," Nicole said, rubbing her forehead with the palm of her right hand.

"As a matter of fact, you're helping. We are back to recycling the kill and using the meat to feed the town, just like we did when Gary owned the café" Bernard said.

"And to top it off, your husband made your parents taste pretty good," George said, taking another bite of his burger.

The five of them laughed as Monica stepped up next to me. George, Marvin and Bernard touched the side of their noses with their first finger and moved back to their tables.

"Everyone in this town is so nice," Monica said, smiling.

"So you would be okay with staying here?" Nicole asked her, touching her shoulder.

"I don't think I have ever smiled so much in my life," Monica said, genuinely happy. "I hope mom and dad never come back."

"Oh really? Why would you say that?" Nicole asked. "You have been so worried about what would happen to y'all if they didn't come back."

"Well, now I know what it's like without them and I'm happier. So Melanie, what does anyone do around here for fun?" Monica asked.

"The high school kids like to gather on bonfire hill. It is located right where three towns meet, so there are just about a hundred kids that gather there each week-end," Melanie told her.

"Awesome. Nicole, do you think I could go hang out on bonfire hill with the other kids?" Monica asked me.

"Sure. Once your shift is over, you can go," Nicole told her, shrugging.

"I can take you over there, if that's okay with Nicole," Melanie said.

"Yeah, that's fine with me. I can send Armando to get you around midnight," Nicole told Monica.

"Midnight? Really?" Monica said, bouncing on her toes and clapping her fingertips together.

"For now, we need to work and finish the day," Nicole told her smiling.

"Right, we are open until nine and I will be here for you until you tell me that I am no longer needed," Monica said.

Nicole placed one hand on her sister's shoulder. "You will be gone way before nine. I want you to be happy and have fun."

"Excuse me! Does anyone work here?" a shrill voice yelled across the restaurant.

Eleven

Everyone in the café turned to glare at the woman who had yelled across the room. The chatter silenced and the only sound that could be heard was the sizzle of the grill.

"Hello! Can I get some service over here!" the shrill voice cut through the silence.

Nicole looked in the direction where the shouting was coming from. A woman had stood up on the bench seat of one of the tables and was waving her arms over her head, trying to get someone's attention.

"What the fuck is happening?" Nicole asked, glaring at the woman.

"That's the bitch," Melanie said, slapping her hand down on the counter in front of me, breaking my piercing eye contact with the woman.

Nicole was looking at Melanie and smirking. "Oh, I'm going to enjoy this." She turned her focus back to the lady, who continued to wave her arms over her head, and make sure to use her customer service tone when she addressed her. "I'm sorry, ma'am. We can take your order here at the counter."

"I don't think so. If you want to work in a restaurant, you need to wait on the customers. That's why you people are called waiters," the lady responded, pounding her fists onto her hips.

"Here at the Roadkill Café, you place your order at the counter, fill your drink at the fountain machine, then we will call your number when your food is ready and you pick it up here at the counter. We offer a fixin's bar, so you can dress your burger however you like," Nicole told her with a cheery tone.

"Not only that, but I believe they prefer to be called servers, not waiters," Melanie chimed in.

"No, you come over here to my table and take my order. That way you can SERVE me," the lady screeched, looking from Nicole to Melanie.

"Ma'am, I am not going to continue shouting across the room with you. If you would like to order, please walk over here to the counter," Nicole told her, continuing to keep the customer service tone in her voice.

"This entire town is full of inbred hicks. Does anyone know how to run a business?" the lady said, stepping down off the bench seat.

She audibly sighed, then headed up to the counter. Nicole stepped between Monica and the register, so she could deal with the unreasonable patron. All the other customers returned to their conversations.

"Welcome to the Roadkill Café. You kill it, we grill it," Nicole greeted her with a forced smile.

"Don't be crass young lady. What kind of hick town

has only one restaurant and the employees don't even serve their customers at their table?" the lady said, pointing her boney finger in Nicole's face.

"I'm sorry you feel that way. Here at the Roadkill Café, orders are taken at the counter," Nicole explained, again.

"And according to your chalkboard menu, all you have is hamburgers. I would prefer a single grilled chicken breast with a caprice salad," the lady demanded, stomping her foot.

"Over to your right, we have a fixin's bar. There is lettuce, tomatoes and I can get you some cheese if you like. Also, the cook could probably scrounge up a piece of meat and grill it into looking like a chicken breast," Nicole told her, still smiling and tilting her head to the side.

"Don't patronize me. I want to speak to the owner of this establishment," the lady said, stomping her foot again.

"I can arrange that, but I don't think you're going to get the response you are looking for," Nicole told her, smirking.

"Just…get…me…the…owner," she said, clapping her hands between words.

"Okay." Nicole turned her back to the customer, then turned around to face her. "Hello, my name is Nicole. I'm the owner of this quaint, small town café. Is there something I can do for you?"

"This is bullshit!" the lady screamed at the top of her voice, before turning and stomping out the front door.

"Okay, Melanie. I'm in. Population control," Nicole told her, mimicking the men and touching the side of her nose with her first finger.

Melanie mirrored Nicole and they laughed. Monica leaned on the counter next to Nicole and scowled.

"What is going on?" Monica asked.

"Maybe we will tell you one day," Melanie said, poking Monica on the tip of her nose.

"Melanie, I need you to go back over to the motel and deal with tyrannosaurus bitch," Fran, the assistant at the motel, said with clenched fists, as she stormed into the restaurant.

"What happened?" Melanie asked.

"She came rushing into the office, demanding that I get her a grilled chicken breast with a caprice salad. I told her that we don't offer room service. Then she told me to get off my lazy ass and go fetch it for her. I told her to wait in her room, then I locked up the office and came over here. I'm not a dog. I don't fucking fetch." Fran plopped down on a seat nearest to the front counter.

"Let me go deal with this," Melanie told Nicole, rolling her eyes, then turning to Fran. "I have something in mind."

Melanie walked to the back of the café and spoke to Armando. Nicole watched through the food window as Armando nodded. He stepped into the freezer and came out with a piece of meat. As he placed it onto the grill, Nicole pointed and furrowed her brow.

"Chicken?" he said, as a question more than an answer and shrugged.

Nicole silently laughed and tossed her head back, as if he had just told the funniest joke. Melanie sliced a tomato, stacked the slices into a pyramid in a styrofoam box, then placed some mozzarella cheese around the tomatoes. She topped it off with chopped basil and pepper.

After placing the box into a bag, Armando retrieved a smaller styrofoam box and boxed up the piece of grilled meat. Melanie placed the second box on top of the other inside the bag, then headed out of the kitchen. She held the bag up at her shoulder, as she walked passed the counter and out the door.

"I don't know what he made for that bitch, but I hope it's poisoned. If I have to come into contact with her again, I might actually punch her in the face," Fran said, dramatically burying her face into her arms on the table.

"I'm not sure what it was either. We have ground beef back there. I don't know how he was able to scrounge up a slice of white meat," Nicole said.

Nicole patted Monica on her shoulder and headed to the kitchen. Since Armando is the one who took care of the dissection of the bodies, Nicole wanted to know what part of them was being passed off as grilled chicken.

"Hey, babe. How's it going out there?" Armando

asked, kissing his wife's forehead.

"What did you make for the raging bitch who wanted the chicken?" Nicole wanted to know.

"Organ meat," he said, laughing.

"Which organ?"

"I don't know. Lung, pancreas, spleen. I just grabbed one that I figured would look the most like chicken from the grill."

"What happens if it doesn't taste like chicken?"

"I don't give a shit. That bitch was screaming about pretentious food and being rude to everyone here. I hope she chokes on a piece of that organ."

"Me too, but I wouldn't say that out loud," Nicole told him, smirking.

"Melanie says I should talk to George, from the general store, about disposal. Apparently he would like to be involved in the transportation process," Armando said, as he cleaned up after the lunch rush.

"Yeah. He was telling me what role he used to play in the process with Gary, when he owned the café. Now he wants to help us in the same way."

"Not only that, but since we have finished with your

parents, now you can assist Melanie and the other guys will do the rest with me."

"Thank goodness. It was really difficult dismembering the bodies and I would prefer to leave it to the guys."

"No problem. Go check on Melanie and see what the pretentious guest had to say about my special dish," Armando laughed.

"Do you want me to relay her review to you?" Nicole asked him.

"I don't care what she thinks. I just want to make sure she didn't give Melanie a hard time about it."

As Nicole left the kitchen, she patted the counter and pointed at the door, just to let Monica know where she was going. Monica nodded and Nicole continued out the door. Melanie was pacing back and forth in the parking lot of the motel, mumbling to herself.

"How's it going over here?" Nicole asked her.

"I don't know if I can wait until the sun goes down. I may need to release poison gas into her air vent and kill her now. At least that way she can't torture anyone else," Melanie said, continuing to pace.

"What did she do?"

"I brought the food over and knocked on the door. First she yelled, 'that better be my food', before she opened the door. I didn't even say anything. I just held the bag up for her. She snatched the bag and told me to wait for her to check it, so I stood in the doorway as she opened each box. She seemed satisfied with what had been prepared."

"That sounds like a good thing."

"It was until she said, 'I knew that dog could fetch', then slammed the door in my face. I have been in the parking lot since, trying to control myself from going in that room and cutting the bitch."

"Armando, Bernard, Marvin and George are discussing disposal. I do have a question though. Does Fran know?" Nicole asked.

Melanie stopped pacing and stood in front of me. "Fran knows about as much as the rest of the town folk. Sometimes tourists come to town and just disappear. They don't ask any questions and the four of us that are involved, don't offer the information," Melanie explained.

"I thought you said everyone in this town knew about this?"

"No, I said the people in this town are different. They believe in population control. Also, they liked the taste of the meat that Gary produced and all we are trying to do is reproduce the flavor."

Twelve

ater that night, three hours before the café closed, Melanie took Monica to the bonfire hill, while after the café closed Armando and Nicole cleaned up for the night. Bernard and Marvin had stopped by to help Armando in the kitchen with preparing for the next meat shipment. George showed up shortly before Melanie returned. He remained out in the café parking lot and was sitting in his truck, watching the motel across the street. He was keeping an eye on bitchzilla, making sure she didn't leave.

"Hey, babe," Nicole shouted from the register area, through the food window, into the kitchen.

"Yeah, what's up?" Armando answered.

"I'm done out here and Melanie wanted to show me the ins and outs to the secret doors from the office to room number one at the motel," Nicole told him.

"Have fun babe. I would say catch me a big one, but I know that's not the case," Armando said, scoffing.

Nicole rolled her eyes at her husband's lame attempt at a joke, then headed out of the café. She waved at George as she walked through the parking lot. He rolled down the window to his truck and beckoned me to approach.

"What's up George?" Nicole said, as she got closer.

"Three others have entered the motel room in the past thirty minutes. One other woman and two guys. We may need to change how this is going to go," George told her.

"I think Melanie should knock on the door to see if they need anything, just to gauge the others. Maybe we could eliminate four shitty people in one go," Nicole told him, shrugging.

"That sounds great. Here she comes. Let's ask her," George said, pointing down the road at the vehicle headed toward them.

Nicole stepped away from George's truck, as the vehicle pulled up and parked two spaces away from where she was standing. Melanie exited the vehicle and joined them. George explained the situation to her. Melanie's face lit up, as the corners of her mouth curled up slowly into a smile and she began rubbing her hands together like a super villain.

"I got this," Melanie said winking, before she skipped across the road toward the motel.

Nicole walked around the truck and opened the passenger side door, before climbing in next to George. The office of the motel was a thousand square foot building with a line of ten rooms to the right of the office. There was a row of ten rooms backed up to the ten that could be seen from the café. Behind that building was another building with the same amount of rooms. There was a slight alleyway between the buildings, but none of it could be used for parking. Some people tried to park there, but Melanie was quick to call the tow company.

George and Nicole watched as Melanie knocked on the door to the first motel room next to the office. The woman who opened the door, was not the woman who threw a fit in the café.

As Melanie stood in the doorway speaking to those inside the room, her stance became more and more defensive. After a few moments, both women from inside the room were standing in front of Melanie. They were angry and Nicole could hear both of them screaming at Melanie from across the street.

Nicole opened the door to the truck, but before she could get out, George grabbed her arm and shook his head. Leaving the passenger door open, she stayed in the truck and continued watching the interaction through the windshield.

Melanie stepped back a couple of steps when the men joined the ladies in the door way. The four inside the room were shouting at Melanie and increasing in aggressiveness. When the lady who threw a fit in the café slapped Melanie across the face, Nicole exited the truck and ran across the street.

"What the hell is going on?" Nicole yelled, as she approached.

"This bitch just knocked on our room door for nothing!" one of the men shouted, from behind the two women.

"I was just making sure you had everything you needed," Melanie said, dramatically grasping the side of her face, pretending to be meek.

"Bullshit! You came over to find out who was in the room with me," the original lady said.

"Look, you were very clear at lunch that you prefer a specific diet. I'm sure that Melanie was making sure you were able to find something for dinner in another town," Nicole calmly stated.

"No, she asked if we needed anything that she could get for us. That to me says she is being nosy about the people I allowed into my room. I paid for this room and I can have whoever I want in my room," the lady argued.

"I'm sorry I bothered you. I am willing to comp an extra night if you would like, as my apology to you," Melanie said, calmly.

"I'm close to asking for a refund. This is harassment," the lady said, pointing her finger in Melanie's face.

"I apologize for bothering you. Y'all have a great night," Nicole told them, ushering Melanie toward the motel office.

Melanie unlocked the door to the office, as the door to the lady's motel room slammed shut. By the time we were in the office, Melanie was laughing.

"What is so funny?" Nicole asked.

"Oh my God. Did you see how pissed they all were?" Melanie asked, laughing so hard she could barely understand her words.

"What did you say to them?" Nicole asked her.

"I just asked if they were going to need extra towels or sheets. It was my way of indirectly asking if the other three were going to be staying overnight and if all of them were going to be engaging in coitus. Plus, I wanted to get a reaction out of all four of them. If the three new people were nice, I was going to abort mission tonight," Melanie told her.

"Okay, well now that we know all four of them are shitty human beings, what is the new plan?"

"There are two ways we can play this. I have remote locks on that room. I can lock the door in order for them to not be able to get out. Once they realize they are locked in, that's when George, Marvin and Bernard go in and terrify them. Although, we might need assistance from Armando as well. As soon as they begin pleading for their lives, that's when we go in and eliminate them while the guys hold them."

"That's one way. What's the other?"

"The other way, we can bang on the door and hide before they open the door. After a few times, they will be so pissed off that they will emerge from the room. Once all four of them are out of the room, then George, Marvin, Bernard and Armando take them down in the parking lot, by slicing their throats. The two of us, then cover the bodies with a sheet, as George runs across the street and gets his truck. He will drive his truck over here and gather the bodies into the back. He will drive the truck around the back of the café and the four guys will unload the bodies to do what needs to be done for disposal," Melanie explained.

"I prefer plan A. Plan B sounds like we could get caught. Where are their vehicles?" Nicole asked.

"The woman arrived in a cab and I can only assume the others did as well. That's easier on me, because we don't have to worry about getting rid of their cars. So, how did you want this to go?"

"I say we go with the first option. Keeping them trapped in the room will ensure that none of them escape. Also, if they are out in the parking lot, we risk the problem of someone spotting the bodies before we are able to load them up in George's truck."

"Sounds good to me. I would rather be more involved in the kill anyway. It would just be a sense of satisfaction to plunge a knife into that twat's neck," Melanie said.

She walked into another room through a door in the back wall, about three feet behind the check-in counter. Nicole followed behind her and found a wall of surveillance cameras from several rooms. There were several buttons on the desk just below the surveillance monitors. Melanie pressed one of the buttons, then turned around to face Nicole.

"Okay, they are now locked in. At this point, we are just going to wait," Melanie told Nicole, sitting down in the office chair.

"Are the guys going to come over here, or are you going to have to call them to let them know when you are ready?" Nicole asked.

"Once the kitchen is prepped to cut up the bodies, they will make their way over here. We may need to request for them to bring Armando with them."

"So what do we do until then?"

"Just watch," Melanie said, pointing at one of the monitors.

Nicole watched the four victims, like a voyeur, as they sat around the room playing card games. The women were topless and allowing it to all hang out, as the men randomly reached over and fondled their breasts.

Thirteen

Melanie and Nicole watched the monitors for about fifteen minutes. By that time they were all naked and they were intertwining their bodies on the single bed in the center of the room. At some point, one of the guys stood up and grabbed the ice bucket before heading toward the door. That was when they noticed the door was locked and they were unable to get out. The others stood from the bed and each tried opening the door to the room. The two of them could see the people yelling, but the sound was turned off.

"I want to hear what they are saying," Nicole told Melanie.

She reached under the desk and pressed a button. Instantly, they could hear the chaos ensuing from inside the room.

"How do we get out of here? Call the motel office," one lady said.

"The phone isn't working," the other lady said, slamming down the receiver to the phone on the bedside table.

"Get out of the way," one guy told the woman trying to open the door.

She moved over to the bed as the man stepped back a few steps from the door. He prepared himself and ran full speed at the door. As his whole body slammed against the solid wood, he practically bounced off and landed hard on his back on the floor.

"Damn, did you see that?" Melanie said, laughing

hysterically. "He flew back like two feet. Not only that, but the door opens into the room so what he just did wouldn't have accomplished what he was hoping for."

As the four hostages huddled on the floor, there was a loud banging on the outside of the motel door, which startled them and both women screamed. Melanie continued to laugh, as Nicole began to evaluate the situation she decided to be included in. Initially, she just wanted to get rid of her parents in order to save her siblings, but she was beginning to realize that Melanie actually found joy in tormenting people.

"Oh man. Did you hear them scream when I banged on the door," Bernard laughed, as he entered the motel office.

"We did and it was absolutely amazing," Melanie told him, swiveling around in the chair to look at him.

"Nicole, are you okay?" George asked, as he entered behind Bernard with Marvin and Armando.

Melanie and Bernard continued laughing and Nicole was quietly glaring at the surveillance monitors. She knew her facial expressions could always give away how she felt and George must have noticed her horrified expression.

"I'm okay," Nicole said, nervously smiling.

"Do you want to go back over to the café and wait for us to return? That would be after we slaughter the meat." Melanie asked, as she leaned back in the chair.

"No. I want to be a part of this," Nicole told her, taking a deep breath.

Growing up, Nicole never felt included in her family. Jessica always made her feel as though she was a burden. She was never included in family movie night and the day she turned fifteen, she was forced to get a job. By the time she was sixteen, she was forced to get a second job due to the fact that Jerry suspected Jessica was having an affair while he was at work. He quit his job in order to stay home and keep an eye on Jessica during the day, so Nicole was left to pay the bills and miss family get togethers.

Even though she was being included in the murder and dismemberment of several people, Melanie, Bernard, Marvin and George actually wanted her to be included. Nicole shook off her apprehension and decided to imagine this as an interactive family game.

"If you want, Nicole, you can stay here and watch from the monitors. That way you can get an idea of what goes on in the next room," Bernard mentioned.

Nicole shook her head. "I was able to slit my mother's throat without a second thought. There is four of them and six of us. Melanie and I can slit their throats while you guys restrain them."

"I'm so glad that you want to be a part of this. Bernard, Marvin, George and I have the closest bond in the town and I would love to add a sister to the group," Melanie said, standing and draping her arm over Nicole's shoulders.

"I just appreciate that y'all have accepted me and my husband in the town. Now, let's get rid of these horrible people," Nicole said, pointing at the monitor.

One guy was in the bathroom, trying to get the two by two and a half foot window open. Even if he was able to open it, none of them could fit through. The other guy punched the large front window a couple of times, before recoiling and clutching his hand to his chest.

"That window is bullet proof. He probably broke

his hand. Also, that bathroom window was superglued and nailed shut years ago," Melanie said, laughing.

"If that guy broke his hand he is less likely to be able to defend himself. Makes it easier on us," Bernard said, grabbing a paper shopping bag from the corner of the room.

Bernard reached into the bag and pulled out several pieces of black cloth. He passed the bag to George and he pulled out the same as Bernard. Melanie took the bag and passed out the remaining contents. There were several ski masks, long sleeve t-shirts, pants and gloves.

"The medium shirts are for us, the extra large are for the guys. The pants have a stretchy waistband, so a medium should fit us all," Melanie told Nicole.

"We normally just layer it on top of our clothes, but I'm wearing cargo pants today and they are too bulky to be underneath another pair of pants," Bernard said, pulling his pants down around his ankles.

"I'm so glad that you chose to wear underwear to-day, Bernard," Marvin said, giggling.

"Hey, I generally wear underwear when we are go-ing hunting. I only go commando on a regular day,"

Bernard said, smiling proudly.

"Anyway, there is another room back there in the dark part of the room. I prefer not to put these clothes over what I'm already wearing. Come on, Nicole. Let's go change back here," Melanie told Nicole, hooking her elbow with hers.

There was a partial wall that divided the room from what could only be described as a water closet. It was dark back there and Nicole could barely see, but there was enough light for both Melanie and her to change their clothes.

"How come there isn't a light back here?" Nicole asked.

"Because the office is generally closed by the time the sun goes down, unless a guest requests a late check-in. The sun shines in through the window, so I don't need a light back here," Melanie explained.

"That makes sense. What is this room supposed to be?" Nicole wondered.

"It's technically my bedroom. This area will fit a twin sized bed, so if I have to stay here for any reason, I have a place to sleep," Melanie said, as she finished dressing.

Nicole pulled on the black shirt and grabbed the ski mask and gloves Melanie handed to her. "That's cute, but don't you live in the house next door?"

There was a cute little farmhouse built five feet from the motel office. As Nicole understood it, everyone who owned a business in town, all lived close to their businesses. Betty lived on the second floor of her boutique that had been converted into an apartment. Bernard lived in a detached garage behind his shop. Marvin had a single room in the back of the gas station he only slept in. Then there was George. He had a small cabin behind the general store just like Armando and Nicole had behind the café.

"Alright ladies. Let's do this," Bernard called, from the other side of the back office.

"We're almost done," Melanie called back.

Both Melanie and Nicole folded the clothes they took off and rounded the corner, to join the guys over by the surveillance camera monitors. George and Bernard had moved a book case away from the wall between the office and the first motel room. There was a hidden doorway cut out in the sheetrock.

"This door leads into the closet in the room. I'm going to enter first in order to scare them. Once I bust out of the closet, the rest of you will follow and we will then each grab a person," Bernard explained, passing each one of them a knife.

Nicole looked over at Melanie. "I'm willing to just follow your lead. Whatever you do, I will do. Let's go."

"I like your gumption, kid," George said, lightly nudging Nicole's shoulder with his fist.

Bernard placed a finger to his lips, then turned toward the hidden doorway. He counted, one…two… three, with his fingers, then burst through the doorway and into the next room.

"Get on the floor now!" Bernard yelled, as the rest of them came through to join him.

The women began screaming as the six of them stormed into the room, all wearing ski masks and black clothing. They were all huddled together, sitting on the floor. At some point they had put their clothes back on and Nicole was thankful for that.

Fourteen

Armando and Bernard each grabbed one of the guys, as George and Marvin each grabbed one of the ladies. They towered over each one of the victims. Melanie and Nicole both grasped their knives in their dominant fist and prepared to finish them off. Nicole walked up next to Marvin and Melanie stepped up next to George. Melanie and Nicole grabbed the women by their hair, pulled their heads back and placed the blades of their knives to their throats. Nicole chose the bitch that screamed at her in her own restaurant.

"One…two…three," Melanie counted as the women screamed..

"What do you want?" the mega bitch screamed.

Nicole yanked on her hair, pulled her head back and pressed the blade of her knife against the woman's throat until blood dribbled down her neck. Melanie did the same with the bitch George was restraining.

"In life, you have two choices. Number one, be a good person and be compassionate towards others, or number two, be a shitty person and suffer the consequences of your actions. Due to the shitty actions of all four of you, you will all pay for those actions," Bernard explained.

"I don't understand. We have been in this room and haven't spoken to anyone all night," the guy Bernard was restraining responded.

"That bitch over there terrorized the entire town when she first arrived," Bernard said, pointing at the woman Marvin and Nicole were holding hostage. "Then, the motel manager came over and asked, politely, if y'all needed anything. That's when all four of you adapted the shitty behavior and acted very disrespectfully toward the motel manager. That means you all are guilty and each one of you must be eliminated. No one should ever have to suffer the verbal abuse all of you have participated in and now you will pay with your lives."

"Please, I'm sorry. I promise we can change," bitchzilla pleaded.

"Too late," Bernard said.

With one quick motion, Melanie and Nicole sliced their victims' necks open, from ear to ear, making sure the knife went in deep enough to lacerate their tracheas. A gurgling sound came from deep within, as blood drained into their airways and spilled out down the front of their shirts. Melanie and Nicole walked across the room, as George and Marvin placed the women's bodies down on the floor. Melanie stepped up next to Bernard and Nicole walked over to where Armando was standing.

"Please. We paid these whores so we could have sex with them. The two of us were motivated by our hormones. We didn't know they were bitches," the guy Armando was holding said.

Armando placed his hand over the guys mouth and pulled his head back to expose his throat. "Shut the fuck up, sicko." Armando turned his focus to his wife. "Just get this over with so we can prepare the meat."

Bernard did the same to the other guy. "Awesome. Ladies, let's do this."

Melanie and Nicole placed the tips of their knives against the throbbing carotid arteries in each of the guys' necks. Blood dribbled out onto their shoulders. Melanie peeked around Bernard and smiled at Nicole. Nicole peeked around Armando and smiled back at her before they both plunged their knives straight into the sides of their necks. When the entire length of their blades had gone all the way through and the tip of the knives protruded out the other side, they yanked the knives out.

Bernard and Armando released their hold and the guys dropped to the floor. Within the first few seconds, both guys grasped their necks and gurgled blood before their bodies were completely drained of life. Blood pools surrounded all four bodies along with blood spatter on the bed, walls, television and furniture around the room.

"So what do we do now?" Nicole asked, looking down at the bloody knife in her hand.

"Lately, the victims are killed and left until the next morning when George stops by to pick them up. Once he has picked up the body, I clean the room," Melanie said.

"I have already backed my truck up outside, so we can take the bodies across the street now. That way Bernard, Marvin, Armando and I can dismember the bodies tonight. Maybe Nicole could help you clean the room tonight," George said.

"That sounds like a plan. I would love to help Melanie clean up the room tonight. That way she doesn't have to worry about it tomorrow," Nicole said.

"Awesome. I hate cleaning this room alone since Fran doesn't know about this aspect of the town. She's too sweet to bring her in on this," Melanie admitted.

Melanie stepped through the closet and reentered the office area in order to unlock the door to the motel room with the secret button. As soon as they heard the lock slide out of place, George opened the door and pulled down the tailgate of his truck. Melanie returned through the secret door and grabbed one of the women by her hair and dragged the body to George's truck.

George lifted the body and tossed it into the bed of his truck as though he were tossing garbage. Nicole dragged out the other woman, then Bernard grabbed both men by hooking his hands under their armpits and dragging both bodies out at the same time. George piled all four of the bodies on top of each other, then closed the tailgate and covered them with the tarp.

George walked over and climbed up into his truck behind the steering wheel. Bernard turned and looked at Nicole. She was scanning the bloody mess all over the room, before she realized he was staring at her.

"Are you doing okay?" Bernard asked her.

"Yeah, I'm fine. Why?" Nicole asked.

"Your facial expression shows you're not okay. You look scared," he told her.

"I'm not scared. I'm just thinking about how big this mess is and I'm thinking that we might have to re-paint the walls," she told him.

"That would be something you would have to ask Melanie," Bernard told her.

"Where is Melanie?" Nicole asked, looking around realizing she was no longer in the room.

"She probably went over to the office to get the cleaning supplies," Marvin mentioned.

Nicole headed toward the closet. "That makes sense. I'm going to go help her."

Before Nicole could step through the opening, Armando approached her and wrapped his arms around her shoulders. Nicole sunk into his embrace and cried. He could tell by the look on her face that she needed a cuddle from her husband.

Nicole wasn't crying because they had just murdered four people. She was crying because she felt like a true member of a family and that family was formed from people who weren't blood related to her.

"Better?" Armando asked, as Nicole pulled away from the hug.

"Thank you, Babe. I didn't realize how much I really needed that hug," Nicole told him, wiping the tears from her cheeks.

Bernard stepped up next to Armando, cupped her face in his hands and looked deep into her eyes. "You are an amazing person and if you ever need a hug, I'm always here for you. I will be your proud dad."

Nicole reached up and grabbed Bernard's wrists. "I really appreciate that."

Bernard dropped his hands, patted her husband's shoulder, then left to join George in the truck. Armando lightly pressed his lips against his wife's forehead, before he turned to follow Marvin out to George's truck. Once all the men were seated in the truck, George pulled away and drove across the street to the café.

Nicole closed the door to the room, then turned and slipped through the secret door inside the closet. Melanie was sitting at the desk, watching the monitors.

"Nicole," Melanie said, as she turned around in the chair to face her. "You have never shown a vulnerable side to you."

"I didn't know how y'all would perceive me, if I

showed too much emotion. When I was growing up if I cried, or showed any type of emotion, I would get beat. My mother would always tell me that she would give me a reason to cry, then slap me across the face. My father would tell me to suck it up, then strike me with his belt. Because of the way my parents reacted to me, I tend to hold in my emotions from others," Nicole explained.

"That makes sense. I bought this motel after my parents disowned me ten years ago. They basically paid me to leave, so I took the money they gave me and bought this motel."

"Why were you disowned?"

"I told them I was a lesbian and they decided that I was living an immoral lifestyle and they didn't want to have anything to do with me. The family that I have made here in town, is my true family. I stand by the idea that family is those you choose to have in your life and not those that were forced upon you at birth."

Fifteen

Melanie and Nicole spent most of the night scrubbing the walls and the floor in the motel room. Melanie stripped the sheets and coverings off the bed, as Nicole wiped down the rest of the furniture. Nicole helped her replace the sheets, before they collected the luggage and guests belongings that were left in the room and headed back through the secret doorway.

"What do we do with the stuff left behind," Nicole asked Melanie.

"You still have that fire pit out between the restaurant and the cabin, right?" Melanie asked.

"Yeah, there's a fire pit out there."

"Okay, we will set up the fire pit and hang out back there, throwing the stuff into the fire. That way the stuff is gone and we don't have to worry about having any part of them left behind."

"Will it all completely burn?"

"As long as you keep it in the fire and don't put the fire out too soon, all of the clothing should burn. As for the luggage, I will give it to Bernard to shred in his wood chipper."

"What about my parents luggage?"

"It was in their vehicle. Their room has been cleared out."

"So there isn't a trace of them even being here?"

"That was all them. I went into their room to get their luggage and it looked as though they had never even been in the room. I checked the back of the car and your mom and dad's luggage was still back there. They never took it out. It gave off the appearance that they were actually planning on leaving your siblings here with you."

"I can guarantee that my mother would have never left the people she created in order to manipulate and order around to do the things she doesn't want to do. It had to be that they were planning to take the kids in the middle of the night and just disappear."

"They would just leave without saying anything to you?" Melanie asked.

"My father was never really around when I was a child and when he was, I was terrified that I would get into trouble. As soon as I graduated from high school, my mother wanted me out of the house because I wasn't home enough for her to manipulate and control. She needs validation from others and would lie to make herself seem like the victim. Anyone who is happy living their life, my mother would do anything to try and bring them down so they would be just as miserable as she was.

"Any time one of us kids achieved accolades in a

sport, or academically, my parents would never say they were proud of us. They just expected us to succeed because they were our parents. Neither one of them ever taught us anything, because they believed that's what teachers were for. If we didn't understand what the teacher was teaching us, it was because we were stupid or we just weren't paying attention in class," Nicole explained.

"You saved your siblings from a life of misery, continuing to live with your parents. You eliminated a couple of bullies from their life and yours."

"Plus, I no longer have to try and fail with trying to have a relationship with a mother who doesn't really want a relationship with me. She just thinks she has to because she chose to have children."

"Think of it this way, you no longer have to worry about them and how they have affected your life negatively. Bernard, Marvin, George and I are your new family. In the morning, we can call the police and report your parents missing. After that, you will never have to think about them again."

Melanie hugged Nicole, before they headed across

the street to join the guys at the restaurant. Both Melanie and Nicole each grabbed two suitcases and dragged them behind them. They left the luggage out by the fire pit before heading inside. All four of the guys were dismembering the bodies and packing the pieces in the giant walk-in freezer.

"Armando, did you pick up Monica from the bonfire hill?" Nicole asked.

"Yes I did. While the two of y'all were cleaning the room, I left to pick her up. All seven of the kids are in the motel room and should be asleep," Armando said.

"Okay, good. We are going to report my parents missing in the morning, so I no longer have to stress out about them," Nicole told him.

"Are you planning to call your grandparents and let them know too?" Armando asked.

"Yes. I figured my grandparents deserve to know that my parents abandoned their children," Nicole told him.

"Sounds good," Armando responded.

Melanie and Nicole assisted with cleaning the blood out of George's truck and hosing it off the ground outside behind the café. The guys were cutting down the third body when Melanie lit up the fire pit. They added some dry leaves and small fallen branches to the fire. As the two of them sat down to wait for the guys to finish up and join them, Erin walked around from the side of the building.

"What are y'all doing over here?" Erin asked.

Nicole jumped up to stop her from getting too close to the open back door of the restaurant. "Why are you out of bed?"

"I can't sleep," Erin said.

"Are you worried about something?" Nicole asked her, trying to lead her back toward the motel.

"Yes. I'm worried that mom and dad are going to come back and get mad at us for being happy during the time they were gone," she told her sister.

"Don't worry. I will protect you. I will never let them hurt you ever again," Nicole told her.

"I just don't want them to come back."

"Erin, all I want you to do, is be a kid and have fun in life. Don't worry about mom and dad's reaction. Just be who you want to be. Go to sleep and in the morning

I will be calling about mom and dad just abandoning y'all here. I will do everything in my power to keep y'all here with me, so you can have a better childhood than I did."

Erin gave Nicole a hug before running across the street and entering the motel room. As soon as Nicole saw the door close, she turned to walk back to the fire pit.

"Is she okay?" Melanie asked.

"She will be fine. She's worried that my parents will come back and be mad at them for being happy while they were gone. Her reaction makes me feel glad that I saved them from the continued abuse," Nicole said, rubbing her face as she sat down next to Melanie.

"You did a good thing. Now let's burn this shit so there isn't any reminder of these horrible people," Melanie said, reaching into one suitcase and pulling out a handful of clothing.

Sixteen

The next morning Nicole called the police to make a report for her missing parents. She chose to tell the police that her parents had abandoned their four young children. The police arrived within a couple of hours to speak to everyone and take the report. Two officers showed up; one male, one female.

"When was the last time anyone saw your parents?" the female officer asked.

"It's been a couple of days. They arrived Saturday morning for the grand opening of my new restaurant and that night they just left and haven't come back," Nicole told the officer.

"What time did they leave?" the male officer asked.

"I don't know. They came over here to talk and they were pretty angry when they left. I assumed they were going back to the motel. I didn't know they weren't there until my sister Monica came over and told me," Nicole explained.

"How old is Monica?" the male officer wanted to know.

"She's seventeen," Nicole told him.

"We are going to need to speak with her. Are there any other children?" the female officer asked.

"Yes. There are six others. Erin is fifteen, Tiffany is seven, Brittney is five, then there are the triplets. Jimmy, Joe and Johnny are three. All of them were left here with me," Nicole told them.

"That's abandonment and neglect. We're going to

need to get child services involved," the female officer said.

"They don't want to be separated and I will be calling my grandparents. If you could please let the family deal with this until we figure out what happened to my parents, we would really appreciate it," Nicole begged.

"Call your grandparents and get them here as soon as you can. Officer Henson will stay here until your grandparents arrive and will be speaking with your siblings. I'm going to file this report and see if anyone can locate them," the male officer said, as he stood before heading out.

Nicole walked across the street to the motel and brought her siblings over to her cabin. Once they were talking to the officer, Nicole stepped outside to call her grandparents. Before she dialed the number, she took a deep breath. Jessica severed ties with her parents before the triplets were born and Nicole hasn't reached out to them either.

Nicole's grandmother answered the phone after one ring. "Hello?"

"Uh…grandma. This is Nicole," she said.

"Nicole. I'm so happy to hear from you. How have you been doing, sweetie?" her grandmother responded.

"It's okay grandma, but I need you to come down here to my restaurant."

"What's going on?"

"I'll tell you when you get here. I just really need you to get here as soon as you can, please."

"Okay honey. Text me the address and I will be there soon."

"Thank you, grandma."

"Your welcome. Send me the address."

As soon as the call ended, Nicole texted the address to her grandmother. All she could do at that point, was wait. Nicole walked back into the cabin, where the female officer was asking her siblings questions and joined them in the living room.

"Why didn't you tell us that your parents were abusive?" the officer asked.

Nicole turned toward Monica and Erin. "What did y'all say?"

"I don't want to go back with mom and dad. I have never been so happy. Last night was the first night I didn't cry myself to sleep. I like it here and I don't want to go back," Erin said, tears rolling down her cheeks.

"Look, when your grandparents get here, we can decide where you're going to go," Officer Henson said to Erin, before turning toward me. "Monica and Erin are old enough to decide if they want to live with family, or go into foster care."

"What about Tiffany, Brittney, Jimmy, Joe and Johnny?" Nicole asked.

"The only thing that can happen with the five little ones is, they either go live with your grandparents, or they will go into foster care," Officer Henson explained.

"Are you sure there isn't a way that they could stay here with me?" Nicole wanted to know. "We have a daycare center in town for them."

"No ma'am. First, you are only twenty. You don't need to worry about five small children that have already suffered trauma. The fifteen and seventeen year old, however, are able to make the decision as to where they want to live. I'm sorry, but if your grandparents won't take the little ones, they will have to go to foster care. If they behave, they can stay together, but if they end up being a handful, they will have to go to separate foster homes," Officer Henson said.

Nicole nodded. "I can understand that. At this point, I guess we are just waiting."

Seventeen

By the time lunch service was winding down for the day, Nicole's grandmother had arrived with her aunt Courtney. They both looked around the café, as they walked through the front door and smiled.

"Welcome to the Roadkill Café. You kill it, we grill it," Nicole said, as they approached the order counter.

"This place is cute. I'm so proud of you being able to open your own business and it looks like it's going to be very successful. Great job," Courtney told her niece.

Nicole began tearing up because her parents never told her they were proud of her when she was growing up. She walked around the counter and embraced her. "Thank you, Aunt Courtney."

Nicole's grandmother rubbed her back. "You seem to be doing really well for yourself, Nicole." She then turned to the register and leaned against the counter. "Hey, Monica. It's nice to see you smiling."

"Hey, grandma. It has been a great couple of days," Monica said, smiling from ear to ear.

"So what is going on and why is Monica here with you?" their grandmother asked.

Nicole took a deep breath, then walked back around the order counter to stand next to her sister. "Well, I had called and asked my parents to come here for the opening weekend. They showed up on Saturday with all seven of my siblings. That night I wanted to speak with them to try and bury the hatchet, but for some reason they got upset with me and stormed out. They left in their car, leaving the kids sleeping in the motel across the street. They never came back and I have been in charge of the kids for the past couple of days. This morning, I called the police to report my parents for abandoning their children with me. However, the police will not allow the five little ones to stay with me, but I can keep Monica and Erin. They need someone to take Tiffany, Brittney and the triplets, or they will go into foster care."

Courtney sucked air between her teeth. "Fuck that. I don't even like those kids. Jessica has turned them into disrespectful assholes."

Nicole's grandmother smacked Courtney on her arm. "Watch your mouth."

Courtney shrugged. "It's true."

Crossing her arms over her chest, Nicole's grandmother rolled her eyes at Courtney, then turned back to Nicole. "Well, I have to agree. Plus, your grandfather and I are enjoying our time to ourselves. We don't want to start over with young kids. This is the consequences of their actions. If Jessica and Jerry have chosen to abandon their children, then they apparently didn't want them. Your grandfather and I haven't been allowed in your lives for almost four years, so all of those kids are strangers to us and there is no telling what horrible things your mother has told them about us."

Nicole nodded. "I understand. My only thought was that if they were placed with family, then we won't lose touch with them. If they are placed in foster care, we may never see them again. I don't really know the triplets. Tiffany and Brittney both have bad attitudes, but I think that their attitudes could be fixed."

Nicole's grandmother shrugged. "Well, someone else can fix it. If you want me to take Monica and Erin, I will do that, but otherwise no, I don't want the little ones."

Courtney nodded. "Hell yeah. I would take Monica and Erin, but Jessica had made shit up in her head that I'm a horrible person. She bullied me my entire childhood and even made sure to get her friends to bully me too. I have been a happier person since she chose to shut me out of her life. It has actually been nice not having to deal with her complaining about her life and trying to get me to feel bad for her because she always plays the victim. She only hates me because she can't manipulate me."

Monica leaned across the counter. "I hope they never come back. They wanted to have robots and those of us that have a mind of our own and refuse to agree with them are severely abused. Tiffany, Brittney and the triplets are generally drugged to be more compliant. All it does is make them tired and they tend to only do what they are told because they are forced to watch when mom and dad beat on me or Erin."

"Well, sounds like the little ones will be better off with people they don't know," Nicole's grandmother said.

Nicole nodded. "I will let the investigator know when they show up with child services. As for right now, would either of you like something to eat?"

Courtney was the first to pipe up. "I'll take a basket of fries."

"That sounds good. I'll have the same," Nicole's grandmother agreed.

Nicole nodded and turned around to let Armando know. Their reaction to the little ones was not surprising, but she was hoping her grandparents would at least want to keep them in the family.

When Armando placed the two baskets of fries in the order window, Nicole picked them up and passed them to her aunt and grandmother. They took their food over to an empty table and sat down.

Eighteen

As Courtney and Nicole's grandmother sat at one of the tables, Bernard and Marvin walked over to join them. Nicole knew they were just trying to size them up in order to make sure that they weren't like Jessica. Nicole was so happy when her grandmother and Courtney welcomed them to sit at the table.

"Well, hello there. Nicole has spoken so highly of the two of you," Bernard said, as he sat down across from Nicole's aunt.

Courtney giggled. "That surprises me, since her mother has refused to allow me to have contact with any of the children. She has told them that I'm not their family and mean nothing to them."

Marvin sat across from Nicole's grandmother and turned toward Courtney. "I thought you were the aunt. How are you not family?"

Courtney rolled her eyes. "Because that bitch has always hated me since the day I was born and she never wanted me in her life. I was nicer to her children than she ever was and she never wanted her children to like me more than they liked her. If her children ever expressed positivity towards me, the hatred she had for me would grow and she would make up shit in her head to make me sound like the bad guy."

Nicole's grandmother backhanded Courtney's arm. "I wish you would watch your mouth. Plus, don't refer to your sister as the 'B' word. That's a derogatory term."

Courtney shrugged. "I don't care if that word has negative connotations. Jessica is a class 'A' beotch. The only time she has ever been nice to me is just to be nosy. She wants to pry into my life and see if she can find anything to use against me to bring me down. Misery loves company and when she is miserable, she wants others to be miserable with her. Since I am generally a happy person, she could never bring me down to her level and that would create more anger inside her against me. I'm sorry mom, but fuck that twat. For all I care, I hope Jessica and Jerry drove off a cliff and died in a fiery car crash."

Bernard and Marvin made eye contact and smiled at each other. The two guys twisted in their seats and glared at Nicole from across the room, over their shoulders, smiling. As they continued speaking with Courtney and Nicole's grandmother, Betty stepped up in front of her at the order counter.

Betty leaned against the counter and smiled. "Hey there, Nicole. Do you think that your sister would want to work in the boutique with me. I need a little helper."

Nicole looked over at Monica, who was standing

next to me. "Well, she has been working here with me and it seems to be working out well. Is there something in particular that you want her to do?"

"Not her, the other one. Erin," Betty responded.

Nicole smiled at the elderly woman. "Oh. She's only fifteen. She can't legally get a job."

Betty smirked. "I'm only looking for a couple hours after school and possibly on weekends. I will pay her in cash and it is just to help make her feel important. In this town, children as young as ten have jobs. It is just to instill a sense of responsibility within them."

"I can ask her. She's in the motel across the street getting the little ones ready to leave," Nicole explained.

Courtney yelled across the room. "Hey, Nicole. Are we able to stay overnight? These people are awesome and I want to hang out in town for a while."

"Of course you can. The motel has a vacancy for you," Melanie announced, as she walked past the table.

"Welcome to the Roadkill Café. You kill it, we grill it," Nicole announced, as Melanie stepped up to the counter and leaned her back against it, facing Nicole's grandmother and aunt.

Courtney smiled and stood. She approached the counter, as Betty touched Nicole's hand before walking away. Nicole nodded at the boutique owner, signifying that she would speak with Erin. Her aunt stepped up next to Melanie with a giant smile on her face.

"I'm Nicole's aunt, Courtney." She reached out to shake the motel owner's hand.

Melanie shook her hand. "I'm Melanie. I own the motel across the street and help out Nicole and Armando with their meat order."

Armando peeped over the order window. "Hey, don't forget about Bernard, Marvin and George. They help too."

"Alright. That's enough," Nicole said, as Bernard, Marvin, George and Armando laughed and placed one finger against the side of their noses.

Courtney leaned over the counter to get closer to Nicole. "I want to know what the inside joke is."

Nicole shook her head. "There's no joke. They are just being guys."

The door to the café swung open and slammed against the wall. A man stood in the doorway with an angry look on his face. "Does anyone work in this fuck-ing town? There's no one at the gas station and no one at the fucking mechanic shop. My car broke down in this shitty po-dunk town and I need someone to look at it so I can get the fuck out of here."

Bernard stood, turned and pointed at Melanie before approaching the jerk. "My name is Bernard. I own the mechanic shop. Do you know what is wrong with your car?"

"If I fucking knew what was wrong with my car, I wouldn't need you now would I, Bernard," the man stated, putting emphasis on Bernard's name.

"Well, let's go take a look and we'll find out how long it could take me to fix it. What's your name?" Bernard told him.

"Greg. I don't know why you need to know that in order to fix my car," the guy said, as he followed Bernard outside.

Melanie looked at Nicole. "He looks to be about five ten, possibly two hundred fifty pounds. That should stock up for a couple of weeks."

Nicole shook her head before glancing at Courtney.

Her aunt was glaring at her with a look that said she understood what the inside joke was from before.

Nineteen

Melanie checked Courtney and Nicole's grandmother into a motel room close to where the children were staying. Courtney had returned to the café, as Nicole's grandmother stayed behind to spend time with the triplets, Brittney and Tiffany before they were taken away.

"Okay, girl. Tell me what really happened," Courtney said, as she leaned over the counter and smiled.

Nicole turned to Monica. "Hey, why don't you go over and hang out with grandma and the little ones before they are gone." Nicole's sister scowled, then left the restaurant. That was when Nicole acknowledged Courtney. "First off, what are you talking about?"

Courtney raised her eyebrows at her niece. "You're a bad liar. Plus, I know you hate Jessica just as much as I do and I think we are enough alike that you may have done what I have only imagined doing a thousand times."

Looking down at her hands on the counter, Nicole picked at her cuticles. "I'm not going to say anything incriminating."

Courtney sighed. "I don't care what you say. I didn't order a burger for two reasons. One, because your restaurant is called the Roadkill Café and you live in a small town so…gross. And two, your explanation as to what happened to your parents, it wouldn't surprise me if they were mixed in there. Melanie just confirmed my suspicion when she described that dick who was telling off the mechanic guy. It was as if she was sizing up the cattle. Just admit that I'm right and I will help you with that fucker."

Nicole smoothed her eyebrows with the heels of her hands, then looked up and made eye contact. "Okay, fine. My parents walked in here with bad attitudes and acted like total assholes."

"Of course. That's what they do," Courtney said.

"Melanie, Bernard and Marvin told me what we could do to save my siblings from the severe emotional, verbal and physical abuse they were exposed to on a daily basis at home. That's when Armando and I agreed to butcher them for meat," Nicole told her.

"And now you all are continuing that with any fuck tards that make their way through your little town. Nice," Courtney said, smirking.

George must have heard our conversation. He stepped up next to Courtney. "Are you planning to move to our little town, pretty lady?"

Courtney giggled. "Oh, you're a dirty old man. I love it. Sorry to burst your bubble baby, but I'm happily married to an awesome guy. However, we do live in the next county down the main road, so we could be here if y'all need any help."

George rubbed his shoulder against Courtney's. "I'm going to hold you to that. Right now we are just waiting for Bernard to get back, so we can get our assignments as to what we will be doing with this one guy."

Melanie bounced up to the counter. "We can only hope it's just the one guy and not with his family. You know we only slaughter adults and not children."

"You think that guy has children?" Courtney asked.

"I don't know, but if Bernard comes back and says that the guy's family was waiting in the car for him to come back, we have to abort mission," Melanie said, shrugging.

Courtney nodded. "I'm going to guarantee that asshole doesn't have a family waiting for him. He seems like the type of person who may have gotten married in his younger years. Maybe he had a couple of kids, but I'm sure that his wife had enough of his shit and divorced his ass a long time ago. Most likely his shitty attitude comes from the fact that he has to work harder to pay his ex-wife with alimony and child support."

"Well, we will find out soon," Melanie said, pointing at the entrance as Bernard returned.

Bernard had a sinister smile on his face as he approached the counter. "Oh, you are going to be stocked up for at least three months."

"How many are there?" Marvin asked, as he joined us at the counter.

"There were three other guys who were waiting by the car. This guy berated me the entire drive, then the other guys went off on me as I hooked up the car to my tow vehicle. After I towed the car to my shop and looked under the hood, it's a simple hose that needs to be replaced, but I told them that it would take me a couple of days to get it fixed and they could stay in the motel until I'm done," Bernard said, as he rubbed his chin.

"Shit. I better go over there and make sure that they aren't giving Fran a hard time," Melanie said, as she ran toward the exit.

The café emptied out by mid-afternoon, but Courtney hung around. Armando, Courtney and Nicole cleaned up and prepared for the dinner service. Just as they finished stocking the cold bar, Nicole's grandmother returned with all seven of the children and the social worker who was going to take the triplets, along with Brittney and Tiffany.

"It's time to say goodbye," Nicole's grandmother told her.

Nicole hugged her youngest siblings, but she felt nothing. Tiffany, Brittney and the triplets clung to Monica and cried. She kept trying to push them away, but they were refusing to let go of her.

"Stop! I want to have my own life. Mom and dad didn't want us and I'm done being forced to take care of kids that aren't mine. Go with this lady and be happy kids. Get off me," Monica yelled at them.

Nicole's grandmother grabbed them all by their arms, pulled them away from Monica and forced them to go with the social worker. Monica headed to the back of the café to get away from the little ones and Erin walked over to stand next to Courtney.

"Hey, Erin." Nicole reached over the counter and tapped her on her shoulder. "Betty wants to know if you want to help her at the boutique for a few hours each day. She's planning to pay you weekly just like she would an employee."

Erin smiled and nodded emphatically. "Yes! If I can, yes!"

"Okay, I will let her know. She will be so happy to have you there," Nicole told her.

Once her grandmother had helped the social worker with the five little ones and they were gone, Nicole's grandmother joined us at the counter in the café. She looked relieved, in a way.

"Hey, Courtney. I'm thinking about going home instead of staying overnight. Were you going to ride with me?" Nicole's grandmother asked.

"Nah, I'll call Kurt to come get me tomorrow after he gets out of work," Courtney told her.

"Well, okay. I'm gonna get going." Nicole's grandmother went around and gave them all hugs before she left.

"Erin, go in the back with Monica for a minute please." Nicole waited for her to be out of earshot before she turned back to Courtney. "After dinner service, we will take care of the assholes at the motel."

"Perfect," Courtney said, smirking.

Twenty

Six months after Nicole's five youngest siblings had been placed in foster care, a warrant for her parents arrest had been issued. They were being charged with child endangerment and abandonment. Nicole had been granted custody of Monica and Erin and they were so happy. Her aunt, Courtney and her husband Kurt, would come into town once a month to visit.

"Welcome to the Roadkill Café. You kill it, we grill it," Nicole announced, as her aunt and uncle entered.

"Hey, Nicole. Who's on the menu today?" Courtney said, laughing.

"Tall, dark and handsome dickwad is being served," Nicole said, laughing.

Monica scowled. "What are y'all talking about?"

"Don't worry, kiddo. I'm not in on the inside joke either," Kurt told Monica, shrugging.

Courtney and Kurt had lunch at the café, just like they had the previous times. After the first month of the restaurant being open, there were two hours between lunch and dinner where they didn't have any guests, so Armando and Nicole decided they would close for those two hours. Once her aunt and uncle were done with their meal, Armando, Monica and Nicole cleaned up before closing.

"Let's go visit Erin at the boutique," Courtney suggested.

"Ten minute walk, or three minute drive?" Nicole asked.

Kurt looked up at the sky. "It's a beautiful day. Let's walk."

As they walked down the road, Fran came sprinting up behind us. "Nicole! What the hell is going on?"

"Fran. What happened?" Nicole asked.

Fran's eyes were red rimmed and tears were streaming down her face. "The police stopped by the motel this morning and were asking Melanie questions about your parents and several other missing tourists. They decided to take her down to the station for more extensive questioning. Ten minutes ago she called me to tell me that they also brought in Bernard, Marvin and George. Why are they being questioned about your missing parents, but you are still here?"

Nicole shrugged. "I don't know. Does that mean that the police are going to come after me?"

"I hope so. It sounds like you have created a problem for everyone in this town. You better fix this and get Melanie back home to me, or I will go to the police myself," Fran said, as she turned and walked back toward the motel.

"What was that about?" Monica asked.

Before Nicole could answer, two police cars with their sirens blaring surrounded them on the side of the road. Courtney and Kurt grabbed ahold of Monica and backed away from both Armando and Nicole.

"Nicole and Armando Suarez? We need the two of you to come down to the station." Officer Henson approached them along with the same male officer who had responded to the call about her parents abandoning her siblings.

"What is going on?" Monica asked.

Officer Henson approached Courtney and Kurt. "Are you their aunt and uncle?"

Courtney and Kurt both nodded.

"Good. Are the two of you able to take care of Monica and Erin until we have concluded our investigation?" Officer Henson requested.

"Uh, yeah. Sure. Do we need to get them an attorney?" Courtney asked.

Officer Henson shook her head. "For right now, we are only asking them questions. They aren't being charged with a crime."

Armando and Nicole were taken down to the police

station and placed in different interrogation rooms. Nicole sat in the small five foot by five foot room for just under three hours. Once Officer Henson returned, she sat across the table from her.

"A detective will be in with you shortly. I just want to make sure you understand why you're here. Your little sister, Tiffany, was throwing a fit at her foster home. The foster mother had to separate her from the triplets because Tiffany insisted on changing their diapers. Tiffany was told to go play and the foster mother would take care of it. Since Tiffany wasn't able to change their diapers, she screamed at the foster mother, then told her that you killed your parents with the help of the motel lady and three old guys.

"After keeping an eye on both you and Melanie, we were able to figure out that the three old guys Tiffany was talking about was Bernard, Marvin and George. A couple of weeks ago, we were actually able to get the evidence we needed to bring you all in. When the detective comes in, he will be able to show you what evidence we have to charge you with at least twenty murders over the past six months." Officer Henson stood and left the room.

Nicole didn't know how Tiffany would even know that they had killed her parents, but the fact that her outburst caused an open investigation into their murders had her dumbfounded. As Nicole was wondering how they were able to gather evidence against them, a man dressed in a nice suit entered the room.

"Hello. I'm Detective Lewis. We are just going to get right to this. Your sister…uh…" The detective sifted through the paperwork he had brought in with him. "Tiffany, said that she was looking out the window of the motel room when your parents left the motel to head over to your restaurant across the street. She saw them go into the restaurant, but they never came out. She then went on to say she saw Melanie leave the restaurant, get into your parents car and drive away in it."

Nicole shook her head. "No. She doesn't know what she saw. Tiffany is upset that I didn't fight to keep her and my other siblings. I was told they couldn't stay with me."

"Well, I have a video here from just a couple of weeks ago." Detective Lewis set up a portable DVD player and turned it on.

The video showed George pull his truck up to the first room of the motel. Then it showed Bernard, Marvin, Melanie and Nicole dragging bodies out of the room and placing them in the back of George's truck. Bernard and Marvin joined George in the truck and it drove over to the back of the café. Melanie and Nicole went back into the room.

"The two of you are in that room for the next three hours before you emerge again with the luggage," Detective Lewis said, as he fast forwarded through the blank space.

The video showed that Melanie and Nicole exited through the office with the luggage of the people they had just murdered for meat. They dragged the luggage across the street to the back of the café. Shortly after they had disappeared behind the building, smoke could be seen billowing from the fire pit.

Detective Lewis again pressed the fast forward on the DVD. "There is another two hours that shows the fire burning before George's truck leaves. Bernard and Marvin eventually emerge from the front and leave in their vehicles. It takes another half hour after that before Melanie leaves the restaurant and heads to her house next to the Motel. The fire continues to burn. Around five thirty in the morning the undercover investigator who is filming made his way over to the fire and sifts through it. He finds several chard pieces of clothing and shoes. What you didn't account for was the fact that certain types of clothing materials don't burn."

He pressed play to show the videographer leave one of the motel rooms and walk across the street. He videoed all the evidence between the café and cabin. Nicole crossed her arms in front of her on the table, then placed her forehead on her arms. Nicole didn't know what to say. They had been caught and all of them had been arrested. She never thought that her little sister would have ratted her out.

About the Author

C. L. Conolly is an avid horror and true crime fan. Her novels are meant to bring attention to real world issues with a major gore focus. She attends several horror conventions and events each year in order to meet readers in person. To find out more, check out www.clconolly.com and follow on all social media platforms.

When C. L. Conolly isn't writing, she's relaxing at her home with her family and pets. She has one son, a daughter-in-law and two grandchildren. Bonus, she is also a monkey mom to a capuchin.

Facebook - C. L. Conolly - Author
Instagram - C. L. Conolly
Twitter - @CLConolly
TikTok - @c.l.conolly
YouTube - @c.l.conolly